"Why did you d

"Why did you make friends with us? The fishing this morning, the coffee last night? What are you doing here right now?"

He stood, locked on to her stare. God, the answer to that would scare them both to death. She was in no condition to learn what he was really doing there.

Cally continued. "If you knew what was going to happen when you got here, why did you act like you cared?"

"It wasn't an act." He couldn't believe he'd said those words out loud. *What am I doing? Get out of here now, North, before you make a complete ass of yourself.*

Cally stared at him with disbelief. Then something in her eyes changed and she was stepping toward him, wrapping herself around him.

His body responded and his mind disconnected from everything except how incredible she felt.

Her arms reached up to circle his neck, pulling him down closer. Then her tongue was sweeping into his mouth, and he was well and truly lost.

KAY THOMAS

BULLETPROOF BODYGUARD

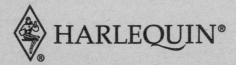

HARLEQUIN®

TORONTO • NEW YORK • LONDON
AMSTERDAM • PARIS • SYDNEY • HAMBURG
STOCKHOLM • ATHENS • TOKYO • MILAN • MADRID
PRAGUE • WARSAW • BUDAPEST • AUCKLAND

To my big brother Tim, who started this whole adventure
over dinner one night with the words: "I've got a story for you…"
Thank you for helping me find the answers to all my questions about
the Mississippi River, casinos, geography and snakes.
But most of all, thank you for believing in me
and encouraging my dream.

Recycling programs
for this product may
not exist in your area.

ISBN-13: 978-0-373-69464-8

BULLETPROOF BODYGUARD

Copyright © 2010 by Kay Thomas

ABOUT THE AUTHOR

Having grown up in the heart of the Mississippi Delta, Kay Thomas considers herself a "recovering" Southern belle. She attended Vanderbilt and graduated from Mississippi State University, with a degree in educational psychology and an emphasis in English. Along the way to publication, she taught high school, worked in an advertising specialty agency, and had a very brief stint in a lingerie store.

Kay met her husband in Dallas when they sat next to each other in a restaurant. Seven weeks later they were engaged. Twenty years later she claims the moral of that story is: "When in Texas look the guy over before you sit next to him because you may be eating dinner with him the rest of your life!" Today she still lives in Dallas with her Texan, their two children and a shockingly spoiled Boston Terrier named Jack.

Kay is thrilled to be writing for Harlequin Intrigue and would love to hear from her readers. Visit her at her Web site, www.kaythomas.net, or drop her a line at P.O. Box 837321, Richardson, TX 75083.

Books by Kay Thomas

HARLEQUIN INTRIGUE
1112—BETTER THAN BULLETPROOF
1130—BULLETPROOF TEXAS
1197—BULLETPROOF BODYGUARD

CAST OF CHARACTERS

Cally Burnett—A young widow and mother who is forced to help with a casino robbery when her young son is kidnapped by guests staying at her bed-and-breakfast.

Marcus North—An undercover cop with a troubled past posing as a bodyguard at the Paddlewheel Casino. Will he choose between saving his career and saving Cally's child?

Gregor Williams—A military contractor about to be indicted by the federal government. He has nothing to lose and everything to gain when he uses Cally's bed-and-breakfast as his base of operations in the robbery.

Harris Burnett—Cally's three-year-old son. Will he survive Gregor's plan?

Luella Wiggins—She and her husband, Bay, help run Cally's bed-and-breakfast. Can Cally count on them when everything falls apart?

Earleen Bledsoe—Marcus's informant at the "Tonk." Can she be trusted to tell the truth?

Asa—Marcus's partner who is under investigation by internal affairs. Will he be able to help Marcus when he needs him the most?

Prologue

Jackson, Mississippi
November, six months ago

Sweat ran down Marcus's back and sides. The heat was cranked up too high and the room was stifling. To top it off, the tape from his body mike was ripping out hairs every time he moved.

Asa had strapped the wire on too tight, but Marcus hadn't complained. His partner had a lot on his mind. At the time Marcus didn't think it would matter. He'd expected to be in and out in twenty minutes. He should've known better.

They were waiting on Donny Simmons to make the delivery, then Marcus could "say the magic words." Of course, Donny was over an hour late, and Marcus was about to melt.

Half an hour ago he'd tried opening the window, but it was painted shut. He considered standing up and trying again, but couldn't summon up the energy.

God, he wanted a drink.

He looked around the shabby little living room. The carpet was worn, stained and smelled awful. Marcus sat on it because the only available chair looked worse. There was an old console television at the far end of the room, but apparently it didn't work.

He felt a prickling sensation along the back of his neck and couldn't figure out if something was truly wrong, or if he was just paranoid. After all, he'd been hanging out with Donny and his friends for the past two months. Some of their paranoia was bound to have rubbed off. He tried to concentrate on something besides the greenhouse effect and chest-hair removal, but he wasn't having much luck.

He knew his men outside weren't in any better shape, except for the heat issue. It was thirty-two degrees and dropping. The weatherman had predicted an ice storm for tonight, but the front was moving in early. Sleet splattered on the window above his head.

Perfect. No wonder Donny was late.

Four patrol guys were in an unmarked car down the street, while a six-man SWAT team was crammed into a plumbers' van parked next door. Marcus had been in that same van last week. The heater was broken, and he knew those men were freezing their butts off as the team listened in.

Up to this point there hadn't been much to hear. Just some dopers sitting around smoking and waiting on a delivery. Three of them to be exact—Donny's brother Charles, his girlfriend Janice and another small-time dealer named Billy.

Charles lay on a broken-down sofa, his back to the room. From his vantage point on the floor, Marcus had a clear view of his T-shirt. Underneath the winged motorcycle emblem, the shirt proclaimed, If you can read this, the bitch fell off.

Charming guy, that Charles.

Janice slumped in a broken-down recliner next to the sofa. Long greasy hair hid her face, and she held a cigarette in grimy hands. Billy fidgeted at the kitchen table, jumping up every five minutes or so to look out the window and pace around the sad-looking kitchen. Marcus wondered what he was on and how long he'd been up.

Mentally he reviewed the pre-raid briefing that had taken place earlier today. He had stood at the front of the conference room in the station house and pointed to himself, "I'll be inside wearing these clothes. Please don't shoot me."

Everyone had laughed and then they'd gotten down to business. At noon the Honorable Judge Watson had signed a search warrant for the property and arrest warrants for Donny, Charles and Billy.

The plan was to wait for Donny to make the sale.

Marcus would say, "It's all good."

Things would roll from there.

The SWAT team would hit the front door, take down the suspects and Marcus would hit the floor. The patrol guys would stay on the perimeter. They should be able to do this with a minimum of fuss, without firing a shot and he hoped, without blowing his cover.

Key word being *should*.

Donny was normally quite punctual with his delivery schedules—very unusual for a doper. Likewise, every Tuesday at four o'clock in the afternoon, Billy was there for a pick-up. Naturally, this was the first time in two months the delivery had been late.

Marcus's thoughts were interrupted by the sound of Donny's Camaro pulling into the driveway. The muffler must be dragging the ground to make that kind of racket. He stood as the dealer hustled in the back door carrying a nylon duffel bag, but Marcus's stomach clenched when he saw the woman with him.

Tessa. He'd been a fool to think he was protecting her by saying *no*. Instead, she was clinging to Donny like he was her ticket to the good life. And for the next few hours he would be, if he shared his product with her. She nodded coolly to Marcus, giving no indication she knew him beyond a casual bar-room acquaintance.

"It's about time," said Charles. "Where ya been?"

"Trying not to wrap my car around a tree." Donny's voice was high and screechy. "It's slicker 'n a greased pig out there."

"Donny, you're such a comedian," sneered Janice.

"Bite me, darlin."

"In your dreams," she retorted.

"Cut the crap," interrupted Marcus. "Let's get on with this. I've got somebody waiting."

"You and me both," said Billy. He walked over to stand beside Marcus. "Let's see the st…"

Boom. Boom. Boom. The battering ram slammed through the front door.

Damn, somebody screwed up. Marcus hit the floor. The SWAT team burst through into the living room with 9mm MP5s.

"What the f—" shouted Charles. His question was cut short as he fell off the couch.

Janice screamed. Donny hit the floor with Marcus. Billy pulled out a 9mm Glock.

"Police… Drop the weapon, you're under arrest!" shouted Tanker, the SWAT-team leader.

Billy didn't hesitate; he just grabbed Tessa and put the Glock to her temple. "You drop it, or I do her right here."

"You got no place to run, man. The house is surrounded. Let her go." Tanker's voice was calm. His entire team was now in the living room pointing their MP5s at Billy.

Marcus was sprawled at Tessa's feet, staring up at the Glock. She was scared, but looked at him with complete trust in her eyes. No way he was pulling out his own gun in this situation. That was a guaranteed way to get them both shot.

He'd suspected Billy was a speed freak, and right now he was pretty sure that the guy was "schitzing out." Marcus figured they had about ten more seconds before Billy completely lost it and starting shooting. If he rolled hard, Marcus could knock Tessa out of the way long enough for Tanker to do his thing.

He glanced over at the SWAT leader, gave him an imperceptible nod and rolled—right into Tessa's calves.

Tessa squealed and pitched backwards, away from the gun. Billy's arm was shoved to the side when she fell. She was safe but Billy squeezed off several rounds as his hand came down. Tessa's scream was cut short. Tanker ran forward and Billy was on the ground before the echo of the shots stopped reverberating around the room.

"Officer down!" shouted Tanker's second in command. "Officer down!"

Marcus turned to check Tessa and see who they were talking about before he felt the pain sear along his shoulder. Fire raced up and down his arm, but his body felt as cold as the sleet coming down outside.

Well, hell. The crowded room darkened around the edges but the volume increased. Tessa lay still beside him, her eyes staring lifelessly at the yellowed ceiling.

NO! Something inside him died when he saw the gunshot wound between her eyes, blood trickling from the corner of her mouth.

Asa shouted for an ambulance and leaned over Marcus, blocking his view of the men huddled around her.

"Tessa?"

Asa didn't answer immediately. "They're working on her. Hang on, partner. Help's on the way."

Marcus saw stark fear in his friend's eyes and was lucid enough to realize Billy's stray bullets might have nicked something major in him. He felt a growing puddle of warm blood beneath him.

Asa never stopped talking as he peeled off his own sweatshirt, wadded it up and pressed the material against Marcus's chest. "You did good, man. You're gonna make Hodges's day. There's a boatload of drugs here. Should be some cash, too. You just stay with me. Okay?"

"Sure," mumbled Marcus.

Asa was lying. Hodges was gonna be pissed at the way this had gone down. Not that Marcus cared what Hodges thought, he'd just screwed up so badly, there wasn't anything his boss could do to make him feel any worse. Tessa was dead and he couldn't tell Asa what that really meant. Marcus had to pretend she was no different from any other addict caught in the cross-fire. Even now.

"I'll be all right," he whispered.

The room grew dimmer.

"You know, I almost passed out from the heat waiting on you guys. Better not tell Hodges, though, huh? I'd really like some fresh air." Marcus could tell his words were slurring and he wasn't making much sense. "I had this feeling something would go wrong.… You know that feeling?"

Then everything went black.

Chapter One

Murphy's Point, South Mississippi
Memorial Day Weekend
Saturday, early evening

"Boat sink! Boat sink!" Harris splashed and water slipped over the side of the claw-footed tub into Cally's lap.

"Of course it does when you have a tidal wave, sweetie."

"Don't want it to sink."

"Then don't splash so much, darlin'. It's almost time to get out—two more minutes."

Cally surveyed the flooded floor. She wasn't sure but there was probably as much water on her as on the bath mat. Her son loved his baths. Of course, she'd need to mop up afterwards.

Still, this was her favorite part of the day. By now her inn-keeping duties were usually done until the following morning when breakfast was served, and she was free to focus on her son. But tonight her guests were running late, so she was getting a head start on the evening routine before they checked in to River Trace.

She would be sold-out with Gregor Williams's group coming in for a gambling holiday, plus her new boarder, Mr. North. She'd never intended to take in a long-term resident, but McCay County was the only area of the state with a housing shortage in this depressed economy. Two hurricanes had recently swept the Mississippi coastline back to back, ravaging an area still struggling after Katrina.

Mr. North, one of the Paddlewheel Casino's onsite bodyguards, was tired of making the hour-and-a-half commute to work from Jackson, and he was more than willing to live here until he could find a more permanent residence. She hadn't met him yet. He'd done everything through e-mail, but she hoped he was pleasant. Even if he wasn't, the money was too good to turn down.

She and Bay, the groundskeeper, had just finished his room today. They'd gradually been converting all the bedrooms in River Trace to guestrooms as the business increased. Moving that antique armoire up to the attic room had about killed them both. But they'd done it, all while Harris napped down here—compliments of her new high-tech baby monitor.

Cally still couldn't believe she was living her dream of running a bed-and-breakfast in Murphy's Point. Of course that dream had come at a crushing price. At twenty-eight years old, she was a widow with a three-year-old son.

Tears pricked the back of her eyes. *Damn it.* She hated to cry. It had been almost four years and the grief could still unexpectedly bring her to her knees. Sometimes the pain snuck up on her like this and grabbed her from behind. She didn't have time for it.

"Boat sink! Boat sink!" More water hit the floor and splattered her shirt, shaking her from memories best left in the past.

"Okay, sailor. It's time to abandon ship and get ready for bed." Harris giggled. "I bring boat?"

"Yes, darling. As soon as I dry it off."

"Yay! Harris take boat to bed…to bed."

Oh, the cry of my heart. "Now let's get your pj's on and brush those teeth."

Bong. Bong.

"Doorbell, Momma."

"Yes, honey. I hear it." One of her guests no doubt. She scrambled up with a wiggling, wet toddler in her arms. *Great.*

"Let's see how fast we can get those pj's on."

After a couple of tries Cally gave up on the pajamas. They were sticking to the damp places on Harris's back, arms and bottom.

"Well, let's just get underwear on so you aren't completely naked." She slipped in a puddle as she stepped out of the bathroom and went down on the one knee that, up to that point, had been dry.

Bong. Bong.

"Coming, coming," she muttered under her breath. "Keep your shirt on."

"Not wearing shirt, Momma."

Cally grinned in spite of herself. She passed the gilded mirror in the hallway and her blue eyes widened. How much water had Harris splashed on her?

Her thick hair, wavy under the best of circumstances, was now falling out of the bun on top of her head and curling around her face in ringlets. Her makeup was completely gone, except for that smear of mascara under her left eye. Her clothes were…soaked. And there was a large wet spot across the front of her blouse that made it practically transparent. *Lovely.*

Bong.

No time to change into dry clothes. She shifted Harris from her hip to her chest and clasped both hands under his bottom.

She glanced in the mirror again. At least she couldn't see her bra through the shirt anymore because Harris now covered her like a blanket. She took a swipe at the mascara and snorted a laugh at the effort.

So much for first impressions.

Marcus was ringing the bell for the fourth time as the heavy front door swung open. The woman behind the massive oak-

and-glass panel held a wet-haired toddler and looked as if she had just stepped out of the bathtub in her clothes.

Marcus started to reach out to shake the lady's hand and realized she couldn't let go of the child.

"Hi, I'm Marcus North. I think you were expecting me earlier?" He smiled.

The kid was wriggling and getting the mother's shirt even wetter and more transparent as he turned around in her arms trying to get a look at the stranger. The woman brushed curly red hair out of her eyes. She smiled tentatively but her corn-flower-blue eyes looked somewhat panicked.

"Hello, Mr. North. I'm Cally Burnett. Welcome to River Trace Inn. I'm glad you're here." She talked fast. "Come on inside. We'll get you all checked in. I…" She hesitated as she looked down at her clothes, clearly uncomfortable at being caught unprepared.

Marcus attempted to put her at ease. "Did you fall in?" he asked with a straight face.

"What…? No…I mean," she stammered and looked down again at her water-stained clothes as a genuine smile tugged at the edge of her lips. She had a beautiful mouth with twin dimples accenting the corners. "I know it looks that way but, actually, I only went wading."

"They say one can drown in two inches of water." He grinned back at her.

Cally winced and seemed to recover her smile, but the dimples were gone. "That's about how much water is on the bathroom floor."

"Well, he looks as if he certainly enjoyed putting it there." Marcus turned his attention to the little boy who was openly staring at him with a confused look.

"Momma didn't fall. She giving me bathed."

Her mouth dimpled faintly. "Of course not, darling. We were just joking. Mr. North, this is my son, Harris."

"Hi, Mr. Nowth."

Marcus reached out his hand to shake Harris's damp one. "Hi, Harris, it's nice to meet you."

"Let's get you all settled. You must be tired after your drive." Cally began the innkeeper's patter as she brought him into the high-ceilinged living room and over to an antique secretary to handle the paperwork.

"No, not so much." Marcus looked around the magnificent room, his undercover cop's brain automatically taking note of and cataloguing details. From the front door he had stepped directly into a large living area with a baby grand piano at one end and a fireplace at the other. Soft moss-green walls made the grandeur much more comfortable than he would have thought possible.

Hardwood floors were covered with several different richly colored oriental rugs. Two loveseats from a bygone era nestled close to the fireplace. Beyond the sitting area on the right he glimpsed the dining room's huge banquet table and antique sideboard. A large rose-crystal chandelier glowed dimly over the table that was already set for breakfast with heavy silver serving pieces and crystal goblets.

A grand staircase ran parallel to the room on the opposite end by the piano. A hallway lay straight ahead that seemed to go toward the back of the house, and rooms connected off each end of the living room.

"You have a beautiful home, Mrs. Burnett. How long have you lived here?"

"A little over eight years." She looked up from the registration book. "This was my husband's family home. His great-grandfather built it at the turn of the century."

"Oh, so it doesn't date back to the Civil War."

"No," she laughed softly. "Although I'm afraid the Chamber of Commerce wishes it did. They wanted to suggest that perhaps William Faulkner slept here. But the sad fact is nothing of historic significance has ever occurred at River Trace."

"Except raising the Burnett family of course."

Her dimples reappeared.

"So do you and your husband run the bed-and-breakfast?"

Again, her smile faltered. "No, my husband died almost four years ago. I run River Trace myself with the help of Bay and Luella Wiggins."

Now it was Marcus's turn to wince. "I'm sorry, I didn't know."

She shook her head and looked back down at the paperwork. "That's all right. It…it happens all the time." She stopped writing to look up at him directly. "I know you don't know what to say."

Marcus nodded gratefully, feeling that he was definitely losing his social skills. He wondered what had happened to the husband.

As if reading his thoughts, Harris piped up, "Daddy dwowned…but not in bathtub."

Cally gaped at the child in shocked surprise. Marcus groaned. No wonder his earlier comment about drowning had caused such an unusual reaction.

"That's right, honey." She recovered herself and held him close as she patted his back and looked into his eyes.

"He lives in heaven with angels."

"Um-hmm," she murmured, still staring into the boy's face.

"Lulu says so. Bay, too."

"That's right, baby. That's right."

She gazed at Harris a moment longer, continuing to cuddle him and took a deep breath. He laid his head on her shoulder. Marcus shifted on his feet, uncomfortable with his eavesdropping. It usually wouldn't bother him, but in this case, it was extraordinarily awkward.

She seemed to sense his discomfort. "I'm sorry, I didn't realize he knew what that meant. I mean we've talked about it, but…" She stopped, blushed a deep pink, clearly at a loss for words.

"That's all right. I'm sorry about what I said earlier."

Her forehead creased, "About?"

"About…the tub."

"Oh," she nodded. "You must be wondering after all this."

Her hand fluttered about Harris's back but her voice was cool and composed. "My husband was in a boating accident. He was duck-hunting and putting out decoys when the boat capsized. His waders filled with water and he drowned."

"I'm terribly sorry."

"I am, too." She sighed. "But life goes on." She looked at the little boy in her arms and gave him a squeeze. "Here's the proof." Harris giggled sleepily. "Let me show you to your room. It's right up these steps." Marcus followed her to the grand staircase. Their feet were silent on the carpeted steps.

"Your room was originally an attic when the house was built. At one time it was a nursery. Now it's definitely the most secluded spot at River Trace."

At the top of the second flight, Cally turned left and led him past several rooms toward the back of the house. Her hair had come out of its pins and was trailing halfway down her back in ringlets. Marcus watched as Harris opened and closed his fists around one of the curls.

The outline of her bra strap was clearly visible through the wet shirt. It was lacey, pink and distracting the hell out of him. She turned right and paused at another landing.

"I thought since you were going to be here a while, this would give you more privacy. You have your own bath and there's another stairway here if you prefer. It was originally a servants' stairway. And if you've had a really long day…" She didn't finish the sentence as she pointed toward the antique one-man elevator.

"It still works?" he asked.

Cally nodded, opened a door and led him up a narrow stairwell. He could see how the location would have been perfect for a child's nursery.

"We just finished getting it all together today."

Marcus stepped up into the room behind her. She crossed another oriental rug and sat Harris down on a wide window seat.

As she leaned over to close the window, he got an unexpected but rather spectacular view of her butt in the water-soaked jeans. Her wet shirt had ridden up and he could see a line of milky-white skin along her back.

He caught himself staring, imagining the view under different circumstances. If she turned around without picking up the boy first, he'd get a peek at the latest Victoria's Secret had to offer. With a jolt he realized he wasn't paying attention to a word she was saying.

"…we painted earlier this week, but I wanted to make sure the smell was completely gone."

Marcus took in a gulp of air, attempting to clear the erotic images forming in his head. "Hmm. All I smell is ah…flowers?"

"Yes." Cally smiled, completely unaware of where his thoughts had been. "That would be the potpourri." She nodded at a silver bowl on the captain's desk to his right.

"The bathroom's through here." She pointed toward the small hallway to his left; straight ahead was a queen-size bed flanked by small antique tables. "We just moved the armoire in today."

He reassessed her as he took in the large cabinetry opposite the window. "You moved that yourself? Up those stairs?" He studied her slim build and tried to imagine her lifting the heavy antique. Even with a man helping her, it was a formidable job.

"Well, Bay and I did. I couldn't have done it on my own. I can't imagine doing any of this without the Wigginses. You'll meet him and Luella tomorrow. River Trace simply couldn't run without them. They're amazing."

"I'd say so." He mentally struggled to get focused again.

"Let's see. I need to get you more towels, and you need a brandy decanter." She ticked the items off on her fingers.

"Excuse me?"

"It's a gift when you check in. Our special label. Homemade peach brandy. Not to be missed." She stared straight at him—open and friendly, but it wasn't a come-on. He knew that.

Facing him, she wasn't holding the kid. Marcus locked his eyes on hers and willed himself not to look below her neck at that transparent shirt.

"Now…what else. Oh, yes. Since you're up three stories here, the fire marshal insists I tell you how to get out in case the stairway is blocked during a fire." She headed for the window seat.

Marcus swallowed hard when she bent over to pick up Harris and lifted the lid on the built-in seat. Her shirt rode up again revealing more of that creamy skin that he was suddenly very curious to touch.

"There's a ladder here," she said over her shoulder.

She reached for the jumble of metal and rope, and he realized he was staring again. He was going to get busted if he didn't stop. He reached around her, accidentally brushing against her shoulder.

"Sorry," he muttered.

She startled. "Thank you," she murmured, stepping aside. "You attach it by those handles to the window and then you can ease down to the roof."

"Where do I go from there?" he asked, keeping his voice as neutral as possible. Touching her had been a bad idea, a really bad idea.

Cally turned to look at him with a sober face and sparkling eyes. "You jump."

He barked a laugh.

"Actually, you shimmy down to that sunroof on the second floor, and then you jump."

"Does every room have one of these?"

"Oh, no. Yours is special. It's the only one on the third floor. There are two staircases up to the second floor and a window in every bedroom. The fire marshal figures if worse comes to worst, everyone else can get out."

Obviously she was struggling to keep a straight face.

"I see."

"River Trace is the only residence to be converted to an inn in the county. The fire marshal had never done this before. I'm afraid he went a bit overboard. We barely talked him out of a sprinkler system. But I feel confident you will be safe during your stay." The dimples were back. "I think the worst thing that would happen if you had to jump is a broken leg."

"Hmm. We'll hope it doesn't come to that."

"Absolutely."

A man could get lost in a smile like hers. Harris yawned widely as Marcus shut the ladder back into the window seat. "Someone is getting sleepy," he said.

Harris was snuggling into her chest and clutching one of her ringlets. "Yes, I'd better put him to bed. I'll be glad to get you something after I get him down."

She was looking at Marcus again with those incredibly blue eyes, totally oblivious of the effect she was having.

"What would you like? A snack of some kind? Or I can fix you a sandwich? Whatever you want."

She had no idea what she'd just said. Marcus swallowed. God, he didn't usually get turned on by unintentional double entendres. "A sandwich would be great if it's not too much trouble. But there's no hurry. I realize you'll have your hands full for the next few minutes."

"It's no problem at all. I'll just put Harris to bed and bring up your sandwich. And those towels and that brandy." She started toward the stairs before turning back. "How does roast beef on whole wheat sound?"

"Delicious."

"It'll be about fifteen minutes."

Downstairs the deep gong of the doorbell echoed through the house.

"That'll be my other guests. Let's make that thirty minutes on the sandwich?"

"No problem."

Cally nodded and headed down the steps. When the door closed, Marcus's smile faded. He looked around the room, taking in the rich red walls and antique four-poster.

This was not the set-up he'd been expecting. Oh, it was quite a place all right. But it was not the proper way for this to go down. What in hell was he going to do about the widow and the kid?

Chapter Two

As Gregor Williams pulled his rented Suburban into the drive of River Trace, the weight of the week pressed down on him. If his lawyers were to be believed, a hearing and indictments were in his future. But he shook off their dire predictions and took in the view before him. Starting now, Gregor had other plans.

The bed-and-breakfast was beautiful, although not to his taste. Surrounded by empty cotton fields, it looked like something out of *Gone with the Wind*—with three stories, red brick, white columns, black shutters and wrought-iron balconies. But what really interested him was how the house backed up to a lake. A setting sun bled along a drive lined with thirty-foot magnolia trees and live oaks that were closer to fifty feet. The secluded plantation home was absolutely perfect for his "project."

"Let's get inside. I've had all the fun I can stand today." His tone invited no argument.

He glanced over his shoulder at the men he'd brought with him. Peter Sams, his second-in-command, was tall, rawboned, in his late forties and completely bald with a goatee. A body-builder and frighteningly strong, Peter had worked with him in some type of capacity for twenty years. First in the military, now for their private security company. Gregor knew Peter Sams almost as well as he knew himself.

A smaller but equally lethal black man was sitting beside

Sams. Rob Johnson had joined their security team in Iraq right before the ill-fated mission that had landed them in their present legal troubles. But he'd proven his worth in that firefight. Gregor could trust his life to both of these men.

Gregor's gaze fell on Frank Boggs next. Sams had found Boggs or rather, relocated his old military buddy. Boggs would be supplying them with everything they would need for the weekend.

He shifted uneasily in his seat. Johnson and Sams had both told him that they were afraid the man couldn't cut it in the clinch. But Gregor felt Boggs could handle his end. The job wasn't going to be that complicated. Besides, the payoff was irresistible. And in their present legal circumstances, absolutely necessary. Gregor had a strategy for making everything work.

He caught a glimpse of himself in the rearview mirror as he swung open the door and nodded. With iron-gray hair and cold blue eyes, he knew he looked formidable. The look was one he had cultivated over the years. He was fifty-two, but his six-foot frame looked like that of a much younger man.

This was his last mission, so to speak. Afterward, he would be retiring to some place tropical and out of the country—where the women wore thong bikinis and were more than willing to accommodate his…unique preferences. He could practically taste the piña coladas as he strode up the paved brick sidewalk.

"All right. Let's do this," he called over his shoulder.

The three men didn't answer. Accustomed to taking orders, they simply swung open their car doors with military precision. Moments later they stood on the tremendous porch at the front of the bed-and-breakfast along with their boss.

Gregor growled, "Smile, damn it. You look like you're about to face a firing squad. We're supposed to be having fun."

Tension rose along the back of his neck. The taste in his mouth no longer reminded him of the tropics. He focused on the large rush welcome mat as he rang the bell.

A stout-looking black woman in a maid's uniform opened the massive paneled door with a smile. "Hello, Mr. Williams. It's good to have you back again. Y'all come on in. Welcome to River Trace."

Gregor dismissed his second thoughts and turned on the charm. "Hello, Luella. It's good to be here. I've been dreaming about your collard greens and buttermilk biscuits for a month."

"You're puttin' me on, sir." Luella's smile grew wider as she shooed them all inside like a mother hen. "Let me get you gentlemen checked in. You have perfect timing. I just got back from dinner. Did you have a pleasant drive?"

Gregor spoke for all of them. "Yes, we did. I'm looking forward to showing my friends the casino. We're hoping to have a profitable weekend."

Luella bustled her way over to the large antique secretary and proceeded with the paperwork and showing them to their rooms on the second floor. Gregor's was the master bedroom with a fireplace and large sitting area. Luella was turning to go downstairs when he asked, "Is Mrs. Burnett home this evening?"

The big woman nodded. "Cally's here. I believe she's checking another guest in. She cooked up some hors d'oeuvres for you and the other gentlemen earlier if you'd like a late cocktail hour. Y'all come on down whenever you're ready. I'll take care of you."

"None of your fried okra?" he teased. "I was really looking forward to that."

"No sir, we haven't picked any okra out of our garden this week. But if you like, I'll have Bay do it in the morning and fix you up a mess of collards and some okra for dinner tomorrow night."

Gregor nodded and laughed out loud, feeling some of the tension ease from his shoulders. "Oh, it really is good to be back at River Trace." He was surprised to realize he truly meant that. "I'm looking forward to my time here."

MARCUS CLIMBED into the steaming enclosure and let the hot water pelt his face. He wanted to wash off the stink of the dive he had been in earlier. His contact had never shown, but he'd met with the people he came to see. Now he reeked of cheap liquor, cigarettes and God only knew what else. He was surprised Mrs. Burnett hadn't noticed, but she'd been distracted by the kid.

Cally Burnett was unexpected. Curvy in all the right places, she intrigued him with that mane of auburn curls and big blue eyes, not to mention those lips that made him think of ice cream and X-rated movies. He shook his head. No more than five foot five, what there was of her was extraordinarily well packaged.

When she'd answered the door, he'd been almost embarrassed by his response. She looked more like the winner of a wet T-shirt contest than a mother and widow. But she certainly wasn't his type. Forget about sex. It had been so long since he'd had an extended *conversation* with a woman who wasn't a cop, a snitch or a victim—he wasn't exactly sure what his type was anymore.

Not that his body's response was any indication; it had no real discernment in these matters, especially given the timing. Celibacy was a bitch. Doing without wasn't his first choice and had more to do with the fact that his love life had been nonexistent lately.

Marcus consciously pushed thoughts of the lovely Mrs. Burnett out of his mind. He had little time to himself to socialize outside of work, and he no longer got involved with the women from this side of his life. It was entirely too complicated and dangerous. Tessa had taught him that lesson the hard way.

He wished Gregor had picked different lodgings. This wasn't going to be as clean as the man claimed. That worried Marcus for the widow's sake as well as his own.

Gregor Williams was a dangerous man. Marcus suspected some mental instability. Boggs had confirmed those suspicions last week when he told a story about Williams "roughing up" a hooker in New Orleans. Later Asa did some checking and found the woman had been hospitalized. It should have caused quite a stir. But for some reason the woman didn't press charges. With the high-profile job Gregor had in Iraq as a private security contractor, a significant amount of money must have changed hands to keep that incident quiet.

Marcus had met Gregor and his mercenaries for the first time a little over a month ago. Things had progressed rapidly from there, once they found out about his position at the casino. And tonight, he'd been at the Tonk where Gregor had spelled out his entire plan.

The bar sat on a gravel back road between two cotton fields. During the day it was hardly more than a shack. At night, with half-burned-out Christmas lights strung around the door, the Tonk looked like an old whore on Bourbon Street determined to sell her worn wares and show the world she still had what it took.

Marcus heard music blaring as he pulled into the potholed dirt parking lot. Three motorcycles and a half dozen trucks were haphazardly parked out front. A light crowd for a Saturday night, but it was early yet. Things didn't start rocking here until after midnight.

The scent of spilled beer, stale sweat and cigarette smoke assaulted him as he cruised inside. The bikers were at the bar with a couple of women Marcus recognized from previous visits. The hookers working here on weekends were a sad lot. The Tonk was the last stop on the food chain. Marcus could never imagine being so desperate to get laid that he'd take up with one of these "ladies." An STD or worse was in a john's future. But, apparently, the women did a booming business—especially on a holiday weekend.

Manny, the owner—a massive black man with two gold front teeth and an attitude—was tending bar. Marcus gave him a nod.

Manny didn't need bouncers in his place. Instead, he kept a sawed-off shotgun behind the counter and a snub-nosed revolver in his belt. Oh, fights might break out. But when Manny told you to leave—you left. The cops were never called.

Heavy metal blasted from the jukebox at the far end of the room. A few tables were scattered around a pool table on the opposite side of the bar, and a game was just starting. Marcus nodded to one of the players as he walked toward the far corner.

Four men sat at a scarred wooden table. Even in the darkened room, their buzz haircuts and perfect posture stood out. There was just no hiding that kind of discipline in a place like this.

"Hello, Gregor. Boggs." Marcus sat without being invited.

The older man in the group spoke in a growl, "North, it's about damn time."

"Here I am, as we discussed."

"Have you checked in yet?"

"No, I'm going over to the bed-and-breakfast after this."

Manny sauntered over with a beer and set it in front of Marcus and nodded a greeting to Frank Boggs.

"Evening, Manny. Where's Earleen tonight?" asked Marcus.

"That girl has done gone and got the flu. Said she might be in later. But she looks worse 'n she usually does." He paused a moment, his gold teeth disappeared, then winked again in the dim light. "She sure hates to miss the weekend tricks."

Marcus laughed out loud. "Yeah, like you'd let that happen. Sure hope she feels better."

"I'll tell her you said so."

Gregor waited until the man ambled back toward the bar. "Who's Earleen?" he asked.

"Manny's daughter," said Marcus.

"Her father pimps for her?" Gregor asked. His growl had changed to a rumble.

Apparently, his few puritanical tendencies were highly offended at their conversation. He didn't get it and Marcus decided not to enlighten him.

There were plenty of tricks turned in Manny's Tonk but his daughter, Earleen, was not involved in that lifestyle. Manny probably didn't know she'd ever even considered it and would kill the man who laid a finger or anything else on his daughter.

"Yeah, he's a real prince. Giving her all the advantages," said Marcus.

"A girlfriend of yours?"

Marcus smiled, but his stomach turned. He'd met Earleen several years ago when she was a runaway and contemplating turning her first trick on Farish Street in Jackson. Working Vice at the time, he'd almost arrested her. Instead, after hearing her story, he'd put her on a bus back home to South Mississippi.

Unfortunately, this audience wasn't interested in the only "happily ever after" Marcus had ever seen while working that side of the street in Jackson, so he spun it a bit.

"I never kiss and tell, Gregor. Do you?"

Boggs snorted. The other two men smiled uneasily.

"You know the nicest people," *snarled Gregor, ignoring the question.*

Marcus realized he was antagonizing his mark more than he should. He slid a manila envelope across the table. "Here's the blueprint you wanted."

"Have any trouble?" *Gregor pulled out a small loose-leaf notebook and tucked the envelope inside.*

"No trouble. The security personnel have access to all the wiring schematics in case there's a problem with the generators or security system. Since I'm a bodyguard, I have access, as well."

"I want to double-check these camera locations against the ones I already have."

"No problem," *Marcus said.* "What else?"

"What time will you finish work tomorrow?"

"Should be done around five-thirty or six. None of my whales are here till the weekend."

"Good. We'll make the final preparations then."

Marcus nodded and made a conscious effort to ignore the

beer in front of him. "Why the bed-and-breakfast? Wouldn't a hotel have worked just as well?"

"Oh, you'll like River Trace—fabulous location, beautiful setting, soothing water." Gregor laughed. It was not a pleasant sound. The other men stared at their drinks.

Marcus didn't trust the answer but knew it was all he would get tonight. He pushed the bottle away. "All right. See you later."

MARCUS SHIVERED. The water was turning cold. He stepped out of the shower, wincing when he grabbed too quickly for the thick white towel on the counter.

He looked down at the ugly red scar that ran along his collarbone. It'd been three months since he'd finished rehab, and the pain could still take his breath away. He'd better take a handful of ibuprofen before he went to bed, or it would hurt like hell tomorrow.

He wiped down the foggy mirror; chocolate-brown eyes stared back at him. Dark circles accented the lines underneath them. His wet black hair needed a trim. He had more gray there than he remembered.

His nose canted slightly to the left—the result of a bar fight when he was twenty. He certainly wasn't twenty anymore. Tonight he looked every one of his thirty-nine years, or as Manny would say, "worse 'n usual."

Marcus dug around in his Dopp kit for the medicine, thinking about the Tonk's owner and his daughter. Apparently, Manny had never delved too deeply into Earleen's "walk on the wild side," he was so glad to have his daughter home.

She'd recognized Marcus as soon as he'd walked into the Tonk—several weeks ago. By her account, she'd never told Manny how she got home from Jackson, or that Marcus was really a cop.

Marcus wasn't sure if that was true, but she had been his best informant since he'd been in McCay County, and Manny hadn't kicked him out of the bar yet. So that was probably a fair sign.

While Manny himself didn't deal, drugs were sold in his place with surprising regularity. The Tonk was a hot spot for all kinds of sin in South Mississippi. Every undesirable, hood and petty crook within a three-hundred-mile radius eventually made their way through his bar.

Earleen had introduced Marcus to lots of people there, including Frank Boggs. Frank dated Carlotta, a friend of Earleen's. That's how this investigation had all started: one interesting conversation at the Tonk with Marcus doing what he did best—listening, blending in, talking when necessary.

When Boggs found out Marcus was a bodyguard at the Paddlewheel, he was anxious to talk about McCay County's sole casino and what it was like to work there. The hell of it was Marcus had been at the Tonk that night strictly to hang before he went to work.

He'd needed to see for himself that Earleen was okay. That she was happy. Every once in a while he needed to see that he'd done something right when the cover was starting to get to him, even if he had to stay under to do it. So technically he wasn't even "working" the job when the initial contact happened.

He ignored the fact that it said something dark about where he chose to spend his time these days. Even working undercover, he recognized he was not in a good place. But then he'd met Boggs and it only reinforced Marcus's self-destructive behavior.

Stupid blind luck.

"So you like working at the casino?" Boggs leaned over the table with his pool cue to take his shot.

"Yeah. Just wish I could make more money at it."

"Don't we all. Lots of money there at the 'Wheel." Boggs sunk a ball in the right corner pocket.

"At the Paddlewheel?" Carlotta plopped down on the round serving table directly across from Frank, seemingly too drunk

to care that others could see straight up her micro mini to a Brazilian wax.

Marcus nodded. "Most casinos make ten to twelve percent. The 'Wheel makes about thirty."

"Good God, what does that much money look like?" Boggs stood up straight, the pool game and Carlotta's peep show forgotten.

"Oh, it's quite a sight. There's a special counting room, of course. A few times there's been so much money they haven't been able to count it fast enough."

"So what did they do?"

"Put the money in plastic garbage bags until they get it counted."

"You're kidding me. Garbage sacks full of money?"

Marcus nodded. "Hell, an armored truck got stuck clear up to the axles once."

"I don't get it," said Boggs.

"The weight. It wasn't a muddy road. It just sank into the gravel because of the weight of the coins. They had to get a damn crane to haul it out of there."

Boggs listened with rapt attention.

"Those two armored security guys were sweating bullets," continued Marcus.

"How come? They got guns, don't they?"

"Yeah, but most of the casino guys don't," said Marcus.

Earleen brought him his extremely watered-down drink, their little secret, and raised an eyebrow when he asked her to keep 'em coming. She handed Carlotta a beer and whispered something to her, but Carlotta didn't respond.

"All that money and no guns," mused Boggs. "Sounds like they're just asking for it."

"The casino is too afraid of bad publicity, like if there was to be an incident, shooting a patron or something. The money's insured against theft once it leaves the casino in the armored trucks."

"Still…seems nuts to me," said Boggs.

"Yeah, but you gotta understand. The Paddlewheel isn't run by the 'casino people' from Biloxi, Tunica or Vegas. It's been an experiment with unbelievable timing. Goes back to the storm. Some good old boys made an investment, along comes Katrina, and suddenly the Paddlewheel's the only casino still online and their little gamble's paying off an incredible return. They had no idea they'd ever be able to compete with the coast or Tunica—they weren't even going to try. They just wanted to cash in on some of the local gambling dollars that were going out of town."

Marcus leaned on his pool cue as he explained. Boggs hung on every word.

"Katrina took those big casinos out just as the Paddlewheel was getting started and people had nowhere else to go to gamble. The 'Wheel earned itself a nice little reputation in the process. A boutique casino if you will. Some folks don't like all the glitz and glam of the big casinos along the coast so they come up here, particularly some of the bigger spenders who like their privacy."

"An awful lot of money to have so little security," Boggs sat directly in front of Carlotta and took her beer. Marcus carefully chose his seat on her other side, to avoid getting an eyeful of her "attributes."

"Oh, they have security. Metal detectors before you go inside and some of the finest manpower available." Marcus thumped his own chest and grinned. "It just doesn't have all the bells and whistles of the big boys' systems."

Marcus hadn't told him anything that wasn't common knowledge. Even the part about garbage sacks of money was already the stuff of urban legend.

Everyone knew the guards didn't carry guns. It's why the

casino had to have those private bodyguards, especially on the big weekends. That was the casino's legal loophole on who could have weapons on the job.

Frank continued to quiz him about his work, specifically security. Marcus answered carefully as the questions became rather pointed.

"You sound like you're planning a robbery," said Marcus.

Boggs laughed and shrugged. "Oh, you never know. I might have some ideas."

Since then, there had been several meetings like the one tonight. He'd met Gregor soon afterward. Asa had been with him for that, but he'd been called back to Jackson last week. The aftermath of that damned Simmons case was still burning them both. Marcus felt it every time he thought of Tessa, while Asa was being put through the wringer by IA about money that had supposedly gone missing from the scene. Marcus wasn't implicated directly—he'd been too busy bleeding out to lift evidence, but the higher-ups were definitely angling to make him guilty by association.

Marcus didn't plan on testifying against his partner, no matter what they threatened. Asa had saved his ass more times than Marcus could count. But they had some issues to deal with when this was all over, starting with Marcus's own confession about Tessa.

He was wiped—mentally and physically. And it was more than just the rigors of the past few weeks. He rummaged in his Dopp kit for a toothbrush as he stubbornly refused to face the obvious. He was on the edge of a burn-out. Maybe things would look better tomorrow.

"Me and Scarlett," he murmured.

His shoulder ached like a bitch. The medicine hadn't kicked in yet. He wanted a Scotch, but knew he wouldn't want to stop with just one.

Cally had forgotten the homemade brandy she'd told him

about when she brought up the sandwich. He was grateful for that. At this moment he might not be able to handle the temptation.

Instead, he brushed his teeth, turned out the bathroom light and dropped the towel before crawling between the cool, soft-as-cloud sheets. He stared at the ceiling fan. Moonlight shone through a gap in the curtains, throwing odd shadows on the far wall. The bowl of dried flowers and spices perfumed the air along with the faint hint of fresh paint.

It wouldn't be much longer. Gregor's plan was already unfolding. His strategy was disturbingly simple and that made it brilliant. In three days the Paddlewheel, the newest casino in Mississippi, would be robbed. And there wasn't a damn thing Marcus could do, unless he helped with the crime.

Chapter Three

"Nooo…No! Help me!"

Marcus sat bolt upright in the bed.

"Bears go away, bears go away!" The child's voice was shrill.

Marcus looked around as he tried to figure out where the sound was coming from. It felt like the kid was crying next to his ear. As he fumbled to turn on the bedside lamp, he spied the red lines dancing up and down on what he assumed was a baby monitor.

"Momma, help! Momma, help me!"

He flipped on the lamp and shook himself awake, puzzling over what the monitor was doing in his room until he vaguely recalled Cally saying something about finishing up the room today.

She must have left it then. He glanced at the clock. He'd been asleep for less than half an hour.

"Momma, plea…se help me." The little voice was sobbing softly, pitifully.

Marcus wasn't sure what to do. He could always just turn the damn thing off and go back to sleep. He was dead tired. But without the baby monitor, he wasn't sure if Harris's mom could hear the crying or not.

"Bears go away, please go away." The boy's cries were low and pleading.

Marcus had heard that tone of desperation in other people's voices before. He'd had to turn those voices off without helping more times than he could count. It had been a requirement for the job.

He'd never mastered the art of being able to do it and not care. God, he was tired. His life felt so…empty.

"Momma…please…help me."

Swinging his legs out of the bed, Marcus sighed heavily and reached for his jeans. He couldn't turn off the monitor and go back to sleep. That voice would haunt him in his dreams.

CALLY SHOVED THE casserole for tomorrow's breakfast into the refrigerator and turned to survey the mess in her kitchen. It wasn't too bad. Only a few dishes needed to be washed before she went to bed.

The large combination kitchen and family room with its stone floors, brightly colored hooked rug and rag-rolled yellow walls was her favorite place in the house. Chambray-blue tile matched a loveseat and large upholstered rocker, both arranged by a generous fireplace.

She spent most of her day here—either cooking for her guests and sideline catering business or playing with Harris. She liked getting as much of the inn's breakfast prepared beforehand as possible. That way she could eat with her son before she served the inn's clientele.

She'd been stepping out of the shower when she remembered that she hadn't made tomorrow's ham-and-cheese casserole for breakfast. Her hair dried on its own in a riot of curls while she cooked. Maroon 5 was turned up on her earbuds. She shimmied and danced in place, singing along about a wake-up call as she washed dishes.

The guest buzzer rang insistently along with a blinking light, startling her into silence. The doorway from the kitchen to the rest of the house was locked at night so the chime rang here and in her bedroom for guests to call her after hours. She turned off the iPod, tightened the belt on her robe and opened the door.

Marcus North, all six feet three inches of him stood there in half-zipped jeans and bare feet. His denim shirt was unbuttoned—dark hair and a washboard abdomen registered. She looked up from this impressive view with some regret and raised a skeptical eyebrow.

Unfortunately in the past, she'd dealt with single male guests who thought a young widow innkeeper was fair game—part of the bed-and-breakfast's à la carte menu. She hoped her new boarder wasn't suffering under the same misconception.

"Yes, Mr. North?"

"I…ah…heard the baby crying over the monitor in my room and wasn't sure if…"

"Oh my gosh, I left that thing in your room this afternoon. I'm so sorry. Did he wake you—"

She took in his tousled dark hair, her eyes dipping down to the unbuttoned shirt again, and interrupted her own question. "Of course he did. Let me go check on him. He has nightmares."

She dashed across the kitchen to the hallway leading back to her private rooms.

"I'll be right back!" she called over her shoulder.

Marcus followed her toward the hallway and stood at the entrance debating what to do. He turned to the large picture window at the far end of the family room. In the moonlight, he spied a boat dock.

River Trace backed up to one of the many half-moon lakes left when the Mississippi River had changed its course over the years. However, this lake was unusual in that it connected to the Mississippi when the water was up. During the flood season, as it was now, a boat could freely travel from the lake to the river and back again.

He looked out over the water and heard a door open down the hall.

Harris's voice echoed around the corner. "Momma, Momma... the bears."

"I know, sweetie, I know. The bears are all gone now. Momma's chased them all away."

"Momma, they...they..." Harris started to hiccup. "They so big."

"They're all gone now, honey. Shhh."

"I called and called but you didn't come." Harris continued to weep and hiccup. Marcus's heart clenched. No matter what, he'd made the right decision coming downstairs.

"I'm so sorry, baby. I didn't hear you. I'm here now. Let's get you a drink."

"Want a—a—ple jui—ce."

"Then that's what we'll get."

Marcus heard them start down the hallway and realized he'd been blatantly eavesdropping again. He headed to the refrigerator and was pulling out the apple juice when Cally came through the doorway carrying Harris.

She stopped.

"Your hands are full," he said in explanation to her raised eyebrows. "Where's a cup?"

She nodded toward the dish-drainer. "He likes the one with the purple leopard spots."

"All right." He felt Cally's eyes on him as he filled the brightly colored cup and handed it to Harris.

"Thh—ank you." He hiccupped.

"You're welcome. Are you okay, big guy?"

Harris nodded, sniffed and stared at Marcus as he drank his juice. Cally swayed back and forth in the timeless manner of women with babies in their arms. Her oversize terrycloth robe fell to her ankles and her hair was a mass of curls around her shoulders. She shouldn't have been attractive to him with her blue-eyed girl-next-door looks. He'd always gone for slightly exotic-looking women in his past, but he couldn't tear his eyes away from her standing there in the kitchen.

"I don't know how to apologize for all this. We don't usually treat guests quite so shabbily."

"It's no problem. I'm just glad we saved Harris from those bears." He smiled at the kid, glad to have something else to focus on.

"Well, you're certainly being a good sport. Harris and I appreciate it."

At the mention of his name, the boy raised his head. "Rock Harris sleep."

Cally smiled. "All right, baby, we'll rock." She and the boy settled into the upholstered rocker by the fireplace. "Want some coffee? I just made some decaf." She nodded toward the counter.

He started to refuse, then looked at the woman rocking her child in the darkened room. Light from the full moon shone on her curly hair and Harris's face. They looked so clean and…*normal* was the word that popped into his mind.

Marcus hadn't experienced anything related to normal or clean in what seemed like forever. Even the people he guarded at the casino generally needed his services because they weren't the most upstanding of characters. There was usually a reason someone would want to harm them.

His undercover work placed him with the underbelly of society. He didn't want to think about how that was changing him. He'd been under too long—losing touch with the things that reminded him who he really was.

He nodded. "Sure, why not?" He didn't want to leave Cally, her son or their small slice of normalcy just yet, and he felt a ridiculous spurt of pleasure that he had an excuse to stay longer.

"Cups are in the cabinet by the stove. Shortbread cookies are in the blue canister."

"You want anything?" he asked.

"Refill my cup, if you don't mind, and I'll be fine. It's there by the sink."

Cally rocked and hummed tunelessly while he located the cookies and put some on a plate. Her voice was soothing and he found himself sinking into it like the boy draped across her chest.

He leaned over to set the cup of coffee by her rocker and caught the lush scent of her hair—exotic and spicy. It was a punch to his gut and another kick to his long-dormant libido that had his head spinning.

She looked awfully angelic to smell so erotic. Not at all what he'd expected from watching her rock the boy.

Harris was almost asleep. Feeling like an awkward teenager who has suddenly found an empty seat next to the head cheerleader, Marcus sat on the loveseat.

"I am so sor…"

He interrupted. "Please don't apologize again. It's all right."

"He's been having these nightmares for over a month. I can't figure out where they came from. Goldilocks is the closest we've come to a scary bear story."

"It's amazing how their minds work."

"Do you have children?"

"Nope, never been married."

"Oh, they're quite an adventure. As you can tell from the evening you've had." He could tell she was smiling in the darkness.

"It must be a challenge, raising one by yourself?"

She didn't answer right away.

"Yes… It's been difficult…and wonderful at the same time."

"How old was Harris when his father died?"

As soon as the words were out, Marcus wished them back. This wasn't what he wanted to be talking about. It was only going to make things more difficult.

"He hadn't been born. We didn't even know I was pregnant."

Marcus listened intently, still marveling at the direction of their conversation. She stopped speaking for a moment, caught up in the memories, he supposed.

"I think the hardest part has been realizing all the things that his father will never see. Harris's first steps, his first haircut, his first little-league game, high school…"

The sadness in her voice didn't reflect self-pity. Unexpectedly, Marcus felt a longing well up inside for something besides the sexual attraction that was coming to life here. He couldn't name it—contentment, maybe. Whatever *it* was, the absence was worrisome.

"We'd been trying for a year to have a baby. I think that's why it bothers me so much…that he never knew."

Her voice wavered and she inhaled sharply. "Jamie and I had a lot of dreams. The most important one came true when Harris was born. It amazes me sometimes that after all that's happened—life can still be good."

Marcus listened to the creaking of the chair as she rocked on in silence. He heard Harris's breathing change as the child drifted off to sleep and found himself identifying with Jamie Burnett. A man who had missed out on his dreams.

Sometimes—when he allowed himself to think about it—Marcus felt that he was missing out on life because he was dead inside.

Could I change? Sitting with this woman in the moonlight, he wanted to believe that it wasn't too late for him.

Cally interrupted his thoughts, "Mr. North, I can't believe I just told you all that. It's got to be more than you ever wanted to know. You are very easy to talk to."

He smiled grimly. *Listening.* It's what he was good at.

"So…what about you? Have you always been a bodyguard?"

He hesitated. Now the deception would have to start. "No, not always." He knew he was being evasive, but found himself not wanting to lie to her.

"I've done a little of everything. But I like security work the best."

She nodded and didn't push. "So do you like working at the casino?"

"Oh, I'm enjoying it. The people are interesting. It's good pay. I like the hours."

"What time will you be going to work in the mornings?"

"It'll vary. All depends on what time my big clients, the whales, are coming in. This week I'm working the night shift, so I don't have to go in until the afternoons. I'll be monitoring security when I don't have a specific client to do one-on-one work for."

"Tomorrow we're serving breakfast in the dining room at nine. If you'd prefer to eat in your room, I can have Luella bring you a tray."

"No, I'll come down for breakfast. That casserole I saw in the fridge looked good."

She smiled. "Specialty of the house."

Marcus sat a moment longer even though he knew it was time to leave. He wanted something that he had no right to ask for. Maybe if they'd met in a different place, under different...normal circumstances.

His timing was disastrous as always. Hell, she'd put him out on his ass and call the police if she knew why he was really here.

"Well, I'd better get this guy to bed. Thanks again for your help. Aren't you glad you got the room with so much privacy?" she teased.

"Nothing like it," he laughed. "Goodnight, Mrs. Burnett."

"Please, after all this, call me Cally."

"All right, Cally. I'm Marcus." He reached out and shook her hand again.

He wasn't expecting it, but when he touched her, a jolt of awareness shimmied up his fingertips and settled in the vicinity of his chest. He barely stopped himself from stepping back. He was surprised at the struggle he had making eye contact.

When he finally forced himself to look at her—wanting to see if she was affected in any way—she was glancing down at her son. He took a deep sip of air. The slice of normalcy was over. It was past time for him to leave.

Harris opened sleepy eyes. "Momma, rock more."

"Okay, baby, but in your room." She stood in the doorway with the child cradled in her arms. Once more, Marcus felt that unnamed longing well up inside his chest.

"See you in the morning, Marcus. Thanks again."

"Goodnight, Cally."

He cruised up the attic stairs to his room to hear the rocking chair creaking over the forgotten baby monitor. He stared at it a moment debating over whether to tote it back downstairs. Cally was singing to Harris.

"Hush, little baby, don't say a word. Momma's gonna buy you a mockingbird." He remembered how she looked with Harris draped across her shoulder, moonlight shining on her hair and the boy's face.

Nope, he needed to stay far away from Cally Burnett tonight, or he might do something he'd regret. He was doing this job by the book, no matter what.

I'm saving my career. What else is there? Too keyed up to sleep but knowing he had to at least try, he slid into bed and turned off the light.

He was reaching to turn off the monitor when her voice stopped him. *"If that mockingbird don't sing, Momma's gonna buy you a diamond ring."*

It was more than the wanting her physically; at least he was pretty sure it was. Hell, he was too tired to puzzle out the mess at this point.

Her voice rolled over him like an ocean wave and he exhaled

as the muscles in his jaw began to unclench. He left the monitor on and stacked his hands behind his head. He'd turn it off when she finished the song. He closed his eyes, drifting off to sleep with Cally's lullaby in his head.

Chapter Four

"And then, to top it all off, I left the monitor on in the attic room and Harris had another one of his nightmares."

"Lord, Cally. How did that happen?" Luella was laughing along with her.

"Oh, I forgot to get it when Bay and I were working in there yesterday. Harris's crying woke up Marcus and he came down to tell me."

"Marcus, huh?"

Cally rolled her eyes. She knew as soon as the words left her lips that Luella would notice that first-name usage.

"Don't get excited..."

Luella snorted. "Well apparently I'm the only one around here who does, and that's just a sad thing."

Cally ignored her pointed remark. She'd been throwing quite a few of those out there lately.

"Then what happened?" asked Luella.

"I got Harris up and rocked him in the kitchen."

"Where was, um...Marcus?"

"He stayed down here to drink a cup of coffee and we talked."

"Um-huh," Luella smacked her gum.

"I couldn't just send him away after he'd gotten out of bed to come tell me about Harris."

"Um-huh." Luella smacked her gum faster.

"So we drank some coffee while Harris calmed down."

"Um-huh."

"Luella, quit 'um-huhing' me."

"Um, um, um."

Cally laughed. "You're impossible. Nothing happened."

"More's the pity. Honey, you need a man."

"Luella, we just talked. Actually, *I* talked. And while I might need a man, I don't think he should be one of my paying guests. Believe me, Mr. North got way more information than he wanted. He is an incredible listener."

"Why, do tell? Exactly what did you two discuss?"

"Jamie mostly, and Harris."

Luella stopped slicing the strawberries and stared at Cally.

"I know. It was kind of weird, I don't think I've talked to anyone like that since Jamie died." She checked the casserole and spoke over her shoulder. She didn't want to meet Luella's eyes. "Guess I've been too busy."

Luella sighed and sliced fruit in silence. Cally wanted to bite her tongue. They'd discussed this before. She was surviving widowhood, thank you very much. She'd sold the farm. She was running the bed-and-breakfast. She was raising her son. She was fine.

She never again wanted to feel the powerlessness she had after Jamie's death. And she didn't need a man to complicate her life. No matter what Luella said.

Cally'd made the decision to raise Harris alone when she'd found out she was pregnant. The wall she'd built around her heart the day she got that stunning news had become her fortress. Six weeks after she'd buried her husband she'd needed armor to survive that wonderful, life-changing…crushing phone call from the doctor's office.

Pregnant and alone, she would never have survived the mind-numbingly painful days that followed without her bulletproof shield intact. When Harris was born, the wall was a way to keep well-meaning busybodies out.

Taking that wall down would be like removing part of herself. She had let Bay and Luella in. They were family and part of her. And Kevin. Her darling, wonderful, gay best friend. Kevin was family, too.

But she'd kept her distance from everyone else since Jamie died—especially attractive, straight single men. She'd stayed behind the wall. It was safe there. Southern manners made it easy.

All you had to say was, "I'm doing fine." No one delved too deeply if you put up the No Trespassing sign on your emotional lawn. No chance of being hurt that way.

Last night she had been astonished to find herself peering over the wall for the first time since those dark days after Jamie's death.

Mentally she scoffed. This was *so* not happening. The thought of it scared her, and that was beyond ridiculous. She needed to get a grip on herself…or buy a vibrator.

Marcus North had been kind, but he obviously had heard more than he cared to know about her personal life.

"He must think I'm an eccentric Southern inn owner," she mused aloud. "Widow with a small child. All I need are five cats and I would fit the bill."

Luella glanced at Cally and snorted again. "Not in that outfit, honey."

Cally looked down at her capri pants and sleeveless wrap-around top. There was nothing the least bit suggestive or sexy about the clothes to her way of thinking.

"Lu, have you lost your mind?"

"No honey, you're just blind in a very good way."

Cally stared at her friend for a moment. She had no idea what to do with her sometimes.

"Harris sure is having a time with Bay. Look at those flowers they're planting." Cally gestured out the window.

"You changing the subject?" asked Luella.

"Yes, I am," Cally answered firmly, but softened it with a smile. "Bay's awfully good to him." She waved a hand toward the dining room. "I couldn't have done this without you two."

"Aw, Cally. You'd have found a way."

"Maybe so, but Harris and I wouldn't be nearly as happy." She stopped slicing the fruit and turned to face Luella.

Luella shook her head. "You'd be fine." Her eyes got a little misty. "I can't imagine my life without that little boy in it."

Cally grinned. "You don't have to. Hey, you said earlier Mr. Williams mentioned your fried okra and collard greens. Why don't you cook supper and I'll clean the rooms today?"

Luella nodded.

"I've got to remember to refill those brandy decanters. I forgot to put one in Mr. North's room yesterday." *And I was so distracted by the man I forgot to take it up to his room last night with the sandwich.*

Okay, so she was interested in Marcus North. Not really her type, but a great listener. A rare quality that Cally discovered she found rather sexy.

Maybe that explained why she'd talked so much last night. Clearly, she needed a confidante. Maybe she should get a dog.

"GOOD MORNING, Mrs. Burnett," said Gregor.

"Good morning. Did you all sleep well?" Cally directed her question to the table of four as she set down the casserole and started serving coffee and juice.

Luella came in behind her and began serving the fruit.

"Yes, we did." Gregor spoke for the group as heads nodded all around. "Just like babies."

Cally smiled. "I'm glad to hear it."

"We thought we might water-ski or fish today."

"The lake's up, so the skiing should be great. Although the water might be a bit chilly." She finished pouring the coffee and began serving the casserole.

Peter Sams laughed, "Oh, we can handle it, Mrs. Burnett." The other men chuckled.

Cally blushed slightly but her eyes flashed a deep blue. "Oh, I'm sure you can," she said with a cool smile. "It's just that the water has been unusually high because of the spring thaw upstream. I'm amazed to see everything that comes down river from up north. You wonder how some of it got in the water. Harris and I drove out to the levee last week and saw a huge telephone pole drifting right along. It looked downright peaceful until we realized how fast the pole was moving."

Gregor dismissed her concerns with a wave of his hand. "We'll only be on the lake, so we won't be in any kind of danger like that, I assure you." He smiled patronizingly. If she only knew the kind of danger these men had faced in their careers. "We'll leave right after breakfast."

"I'll clean your rooms while you're out." She finished serving and set the rest of the casserole on the sideboard alongside the fruit Luella had left a moment before.

"You mentioned fried okra and collard greens yesterday to Luella. If you'd like, I can have her fix that along with some cornbread for dinner tonight, instead of the menu we'd talked about when you made reservations."

"That sounds fine. Sams here has never had true Southern 'soul food.'"

"Well, we can take care of that. Dinner at six o'clock?"

"We'll be here."

Gregor watched her leave the room, waiting to be sure she was out of earshot. "That'll give us plenty of time to check out Palmers and go pick up the boat in town."

The men nodded as they ate.

"Damn, this is good," said Sams. "I see why River Trace made such an impression on you, Gregor."

"Told you I'd picked the perfect location." Gregor stared

hard at the door Cally had just walked through, his eyes taking on a feral gleam. "Besides, there's no reason we can't mix business with pleasure."

MARCUS'S CALVES burned and his chest ached as he ran up the graveled driveway. He needed to run more regularly. He told himself that every time he jogged.

A shame it wasn't going to happen anytime soon. Time was in much too short supply these days. This case was about to reach critical mass, not taking into account the trouble brewing in Jackson.

Hodges and his captain couldn't believe what Marcus and Asa had turned over in the two-horse town of Murphy's Point. The lieutenant would never have given them McCay County if he suspected it was going to be a hotbed of activity.

This governor's special casino task force was meant to be a punishment from Hodges—a you-may-be-on-the-team-but-you-won't-see-any-real-action kind of assignment.

As counties along the Mississippi River passed their own gaming amendments, the potential for petty and violent crime increased. Twenty years ago and two hundred and fifty miles north on Highway 61, Tunica County was a prime example. When the gaming amendments were initially passed, Tunica had only five deputies and no set infrastructure to handle the huge influx of cash suddenly coming into the county.

Today, Tunica was a mini-Vegas. The county itself had definitely had some growing pains along the way. Robbery, as well as fraud and tax evasion, were potentially huge problems.

The best way to get a handle on those problems was to send in undercover employees in areas of responsibility within the casinos themselves. It was effective, but extraordinarily slow undercover work. Because they were on Internal Affairs' hit list, Marcus and Asa had been given what was thought to be the least-desirable location in the state.

Initially, Internal Affairs had no solid proof to stop Marcus or his partner from going on the governor's special task force. But now it seemed that they did have evidence of misconduct in the Donny Simmons case—enough evidence to pull Asa from active duty. The investigation could end Asa's career and seriously damage Marcus's by association. Everything was being examined with a fine-tooth comb.

Marcus had gone back to Jackson last weekend thinking he might take some time to decompress before this assignment got intense. He hadn't even planned on going into the office.

What a joke.

Hodges had found out he was in town, and Marcus had spent the better part of Friday and Saturday being grilled by Internal Affairs and his boss. He could still smell the stale cigars in Hodges's airless office.

The lieutenant had ranted and raved for hours with one of those same cheap, unlit cigars hanging out of the corner of his mouth, his bald head shiny from perpetual perspiration.

"I understand your hesitation to testify against your partner. But hear me now. You are on a very short leash. You even sneeze funny, IA will be all over you like white on rice. Do this assignment by the book or there won't be a job to come back to. You got it?"

Yeah, he got it all right. What was he going to do? Internal Affairs was breathing down his neck.

He'd tried to tell them he had no testimony to give. Hell, he'd gotten shot during the raid and taken away in an ambulance. How could he know anything about what had happened afterward? And regardless, there was no way he was testifying against his partner. He'd quit before throwing Asa under the bus. Besides, Marcus had his own demons to deal with on the Simmons case.

After the "quality time" with his lieutenant, he'd gone back to his apartment and stared at a glass of Scotch for ten minutes before pouring it down the drain. Oblivion had never seemed more appealing, but he'd promised himself never to go there again.

Marcus rounded the corner of River Trace and almost ran over Harris and a rather large black man digging in a flowerbed by the driveway.

"Howdy, Harris. Those bears didn't come back last night did they?" Since he'd left the monitor on all night, Marcus knew the answer to that question. He'd felt foolish when he woke and realized he'd been sung to sleep just like the boy.

Harris's companion stood. He was taller than Marcus, but thinner and appeared a bit frail.

"Hi, I'm Marcus North." He reached out to shake the older man's hand. His grip had Marcus reassessing the frail part of his evaluation.

"Bay Wiggins. I work for Cally."

"It's good to meet you, Bay. You and Harris are doing a great job on those flowers."

"Worms," said Harris.

"Excuse me?" Marcus asked.

"We're digging up worms to go fishing down off the dock," Bay explained.

Harris held up a bucket. Marcus saw several wigglers writhing in the soil. He leaned over to inspect the bucket.

"Those are awfully big ones, Harris."

He looked up at Bay. "What are you fishing for?"

"Crappie mainly, maybe some brim. T'ain't sure if the water's warm enough or not. We'll see."

"Mr. Nowth, come, too?" asked Harris with expectant eyes.

Bay nodded, "You're welcome to join us. We'll just be down to the dock."

"That's a fine invitation and I thank you both. Unfortunately, I've got to go to work."

Harris's shoulders drooped as he looked down at the tops of his dinosaur tennis shoes.

Marcus hesitated and found he couldn't stop the words, "How about I come watch for a minute? I think I can manage a little time for fishing."

They walked down to the dock together, Marcus puzzling over why he didn't want to disappoint this child. Harris reached up unselfconsciously and took his hand as they stepped onto the wooden planks.

Marcus almost stumbled.

"Cally won't let him on the dock without holding an adult's hand or wearing a life jacket," Bay explained.

Marcus nodded his understanding and they continued to the end of the pier. Harris tugged on his hand indicating he wanted to sit by him. It was an unfamiliar but not unwelcome circumstance.

Bay baited a hook while Harris jumped up, clapping and giggling—effectively scaring off every fish within a hundred-yard radius. But Bay never said a word. He just sat and helped Harris get a grip on the pole.

"Can you really catch anything off this dock?" asked Marcus.

"Sometimes. Early in the morning before the boats get out on the lake." Bay smiled down at Harris. The child was happily clutching the pole, bobbing it back and forth in the water like a maestro conducting a symphony. "It's quiet then."

Marcus sat in companionable silence with the old man and the boy. He was surprised to find himself in another normal situation. Well, maybe he should rephrase that.

An undercover cop fishing with an elderly black man and a little white boy wasn't exactly normal, but it was peaceful. He could get used to this.

Mentally he scoffed at himself. Hell, who was he kidding? When this job was over he'd never be here again. He might not even been employable with the department.

Looking out over the water, Marcus had difficulty pulling

his thoughts into focus. It was hard to reconcile the life he had been living with what this felt like—relaxed, innocent, calm. Harris leaned his head against Marcus's shoulder as if it were the most natural thing in the world. After a couple of minutes he decided to give up the soul-searching and just enjoy the moment—while it lasted.

Chapter Five

Watching from the window, Cally felt a tug at her heart when Harris reached up to take Marcus's hand. When her son was safely seated at the end of the pier, she went back to finish the dishes.

After Jamie'd died, she'd avoided the lake for months. To this day, she wouldn't get in a boat, but she could stand on the dock now without feeling overwhelmed. She was thankful that Harris showed no signs of her water phobia. Still, it was a painful pleasure to see him out there with Marcus, looking for all the world like a father and son.

She was pulling down the stockpot for collard greens when she heard a commotion outside. The back door slammed shut, opened and slammed shut again.

"Momma, got fish! I caught fish!"

"Hang on, Harris, you've got mud on your feet, and the fish is dripping…I'll get your Mom. Wait just a second, oh hel…heck. I've got mud on my feet, too. Hang on." She heard the laughter in those words, and something stirred deep inside her. Marcus North had one sexy voice.

She hurried into the back foyer to find Harris outside the screen door holding a wet, wriggling, extraordinarily small fish. Water splattered everywhere as he tracked mud back and forth with his pint-size sneakers. Marcus stood in water-splotched running shorts and a T-shirt with the arms ripped out.

A large sweat stain covered the center of his chest. His expensive-looking running shoes were caked in mud. He was keeping the screen door braced shut with one hand to keep Harris and the mess outside and trying to take off his sneakers with the other.

Harris spied her through the mesh door and lifted the gasping fish up for examination. "We caught fish!"

"I see you did, sweetheart, that's wonderful. Let me look." She stepped out to examine the squirming crappie. "He's a very pretty fish. How in the world did you manage it?"

"He spit on worm," piped Harris.

She raised an eyebrow.

"Don't give away all the trade secrets." Marcus spoke in a stage whisper.

Harris giggled and Marcus continued. "It was skill and fishing prowess. Of course, I think it also helped that the fish is stone deaf."

"Undoubtedly. Well, you two must be terribly hungry after battling such a worthy opponent. Would you like some breakfast?"

"Not hungry," said Harris. "Want show fish to Lulu."

"Oh, I'm sure she'd love to see it, dear." She wondered where the fish would end up as Bay lumbered around the side of the carport. "Why don't you let Bay help you? He'll make sure Luella gets to see it."

"I'll take care of it," said Bay. "Boy, come help me put away the poles."

She mouthed a silent *Thank you* over Harris's head.

"'Kay. Bye, Mr. Nowth. Thank you." Harris nodded happily and trotted down the sidewalk with Bay.

"Well, you've certainly made his day." She turned to Marcus. "How about some breakfast? I can have Luella bring a tray up to you or you can eat in the dining room."

"Would it be okay if I ate in the kitchen? I'm too dirty to sit in your dining room."

She swallowed her surprise. "Sure. That'd be fine. Come in. You can eat at the breakfast bar."

"Sounds great. I just need to wash up."

"You can use the sink in here." She handed him a fresh towel. "So…have you always been a championship fisherman?"

"Oh, absolutely. My brother, sister and I spent summers on the coast at my grandparents'. We practically slept with our fishing poles."

"That sounds…um…interesting? Where on the coast?"

"Galveston. I have a cousin from Artesia, we'd all get shipped to Texas for two weeks every June." He smiled. "Harlan just got married a couple of months ago."

"Did you go to the wedding?"

"Yeah, it was the first time we'd all been together in…a very long time. Harlan's got himself an instant family and a very full plate, and I don't know that I've ever seen him this happy. Ever."

"Sounds nice."

Marcus nodded and helped himself to a cup of coffee. "I suppose so."

"I was an only child," said Cally. "I always wanted to have a brother or sister or both. My friends with little brothers told me I was crazy, but I didn't ever believe them." She placed silverware and a linen napkin beside his plate. "Do you get to see your family often?"

"No, not much any more. We were close growing up, though. Marcus paused just long enough for her to wonder what he'd been about to say. "What about you?" he asked, easily changing topics. "Where did you grow up?"

"Kentucky, mostly. Bluegrass country. Also Florida, California, sort of everywhere. My dad was a horse trainer. We moved around a lot on the circuit."

"How did you end up here?"

"I met Jamie while I was at Memphis State. I was working my way through school waiting tables. He came back to my station four nights in row before I would agree to give him my phone number."

"So you were the cautious type?"

Cally smiled and shook her head. "Up until we went out on our first date. He sort of swept me off my feet."

"A whirlwind romance?" Marcus shoveled in a bite of his casserole and chewed thoughtfully. "And you don't let that happen anymore, do you?"

"Excuse me?"

"Do you ever get swept away, caught up in the moment?"

She stared at him. Completely dumbfounded. "I'm not...no, no I don't." She looked away, flustered, and then forced herself to look back into those deep-chocolate eyes. Completely out of her comfort zone. *Oh, what the heck. What harm will flirting do?*

She looked directly at him. "No, I usually don't. Not anymore. Not since..." Her voice trailed off. She was starting to lose her nerve. "But lately I've been thinking I should change that."

He grinned, and she felt that same tug inside that she'd felt earlier when she'd heard the laughter in his voice with Harris.

"Really." He put his fork down, put his hands on the counter and leaned toward her. "Just what would you change exactly?"

She took a deep breath and fell into his gaze. "I've been thinking I need to be more open to the possibilities of what's—"

"Momma. Momma. Look what Luella made me." Harris came busting in with a handful of dinosaur-shaped cookies.

Cally looked up from Marcus's mesmerizing eyes with an odd combination of regret and relief. "Why, those are wonderful, darling." She glanced back at Marcus then focused on Harris. "Where's your fish?"

"Bay's taking care of it."

"I see."

Marcus finished his casserole and glanced at his watch. "I didn't realize how late it was. This was great, but I've got to run."

He picked up the dishes, set them in the sink and dashed for the kitchen door. "See you later. Thanks for breakfast."

Cally nodded numbly as the door closed behind his swift departure. She could hear him jogging up the back stairs.

The eccentric Southern innkeeper had struck again. She'd bent his ear with the next installment of her life story.

Jeez. She really needed to see about getting that dog.

MARCUS RAN up the steps cursing himself silently. What in the hell was he doing with Cally Burnett and her kid? He must be insane. What had happened to his "cool professionalism?"

That was easy enough to answer. He'd looked at her and seen this amazingly bright, funny woman who'd overcome crushing tragedy, who didn't need him at all.

If her kid hadn't interrupted them, he might have kissed her—right there in her kitchen—where Gregor, Sams or anyone could have seen them. Things wouldn't be safe for any of them if he formed attachments. That would only make it more difficult to do his job.

But he hadn't been able to resist her or her little boy. They were both so open and friendly. No hidden agendas.

Undercover work didn't lend itself well to relationships. He should know that by now. Hadn't he learned it the hard way?

He'd promised himself he'd never let the job change him. He'd give it up first. But that had been rather naive. Of course working undercover had changed him.

So much so that there were days he hardly recognized himself. Then he'd made a stupid mistake that had snowballed into a disaster. He still found it remarkable that he hadn't destroyed his career…yet.

As an undercover cop, he knew the risks of getting involved with a junkie. It had actually started out innocently and flattened him when he wasn't paying attention.

Tessa had been different—sensitive and fragile, but she'd still been turning tricks for dope.

Marcus had kept her at arm's length for months. Several

times he'd even tried to steer her away from the people he was investigating, going so far as to talk to her about the life she was throwing away. But it was hopeless. He couldn't give what he didn't have.

Drinking heavily was part of his cover and after going in deep, his real life blurred with the counterfeit one. One night he'd started on a bottle of Laphroaig and when Tessa came around, he hadn't stopped drinking until they'd landed in bed. The next morning he'd felt so guilty, he couldn't even look her in the eye.

She'd begged him for a hit. He'd refused and he'd actually fooled himself into thinking that was a way of taking care of her until twenty-four hours later when she'd walked into the middle of the Simmons drug bust that had killed her.

No one knew about the night they'd spent together, not even Asa. Tessa's death had saved Marcus's career and simultaneously destroyed his soul when IA's investigation into his partner and some missing drug money had started.

During his shoulder rehab after the shooting, Marcus had got help with the drinking, and he'd sworn he'd never be that out of control or vulnerable again. He was now a machine where work was concerned.

This morning had been a novel experience. He couldn't believe Cally had gotten him to talk about Harlan and that wedding last month. That she'd gotten him to talk about himself at all.

He'd practically sprinted from her kitchen when he'd realized how much she got to him. How much he cared about what she thought of him. She liked him now, but she'd think he was the devil himself before this was over.

Cally and Harris's lives were light years away from his and he'd better not forget it, or they might end up paying the ultimate price. Just like Tessa.

Chapter Six

Cally finished making up the king-size bed and paused to survey her old room. The walls had looked better painted green. She shrugged ruefully.

After Jamie had drowned she had tried repainting and rearranging the furniture—just like the books on handling grief suggested. However, redecorating the bedroom hadn't eased the devastating loneliness even a little. She had felt irrevocably lost and horribly scared. So she'd moved downstairs to the converted servants' quarters.

Since Harris had been born six months later, she hadn't had time to think about being lonely. Today, the ghosts were gone. She was more comfortable here than she'd been since Jamie had died.

She picked up her bucket of cleaning supplies and headed toward the master bathroom, stopping by the antique roll-top desk to refill the Waterford decanter. Apparently, Gregor Williams liked her homemade brandy.

Cally poured liqueur from her pitcher into the crystal decanter. Placing the Waterford back on the desktop, she bobbled the pitcher. She made a grab for it with both hands and caught the pitcher but knocked over the full crystal decanter.

Uttering a series of unladylike expletives, she grabbed a towel and started mopping up the sticky liquid.

"My God, what a mess," she muttered. "Stupid, stupid, stupid!"

The cordial ran down the sides of the desk, over the blotter and into a partially open drawer. The towel was saturated, and she cussed some more as she ran to get water from the bathroom.

After cleaning the sides and top of the desk, she started on the drawer. The inside had caught more of the liqueur than she'd first realized.

She pulled out wet custom-engraved River Trace stationery and was surprised to find a manila file folder underneath, also soaking in brandy. This was Mr. Williams's file, and she hesitated before removing a guest's property.

The scent of peaches was quite strong. The folder was practically floating in a puddle of liqueur; obviously some of the pages were drenched.

I'll just open the file and lay it out on the towel, otherwise the contents will be ruined.

She didn't want to be prying but surely Gregor would rather she saved the papers than let them sit in liquid until he got home from the lake. She could only hope the pages themselves held nothing very important or hard to replace.

She opened the ruined folder and groaned. Inside was an architectural drawing steeped in brandy. She tried to sop up the mess and noticed the words *Paddlewheel security cameras* written across the bottom.

"What in the world?" These were blueprints of…the Paddlewheel? She turned the page and saw another layout of what appeared to be the casino.

Automatically she began blotting up the liqueur. The impact of what she was seeing didn't hit her initially. But flipping through the sticky pages, she ignored her resolve not to snoop. She couldn't believe what she was holding—the entire architectural plan for the Paddlewheel along with generator and security schematics.

She turned the last of the brandy-soaked papers and found another rendering for the lower floor of the casino with red markings. Entrances and bypass security doors were highlighted. A room was circled in red.

Looking more closely at the damp drawing, she could just make out the penciled words—*counting room* and *detonator placement*. Fear shuddered down her spine. What were these men really doing here?

Taking a deep breath, she tried to tell herself she was being foolish. That she misunderstood. Maybe Gregor and his men were from one of those companies that checked out the security in places like the casino. Cally knew she was grasping at straws. These men were military, not civilian.

She glanced at her watch. Five o'clock. She hadn't realized how late a start she had gotten on cleaning the rooms.

They'd be back in the next hour. She'd have to hurry if she was going to search their rooms.

Cally wiped off the file folder as best she could and laid it back in the drawer. All pretense of not prying gone, she quickly searched the closet and found nothing. Next, she rifled through dresser drawers.

Nothing.

But when she yanked up the skirt to the four-poster, she hit paydirt—a large rectangular case up toward the head of the bed. Jamie had had gun cases—she knew one when she saw it.

She took a moment to calm her breathing before pulling the case toward her. The latches popped open easily. Inside were four guns.

Two looked like small machine guns, another was a rifle with a special scope. There was also a .38 Special, similar to the one she had downstairs on the top shelf of her closet.

The sight of the weapons stunned her like a physical blow.

Her mind raced, but her actions were sluggish as she sat on the floor staring into the case.

Snippets of conversations with Gregor floated back to her from previous visits. His questions about the geography of the area and the local police force. Cally had never realized she was being pumped for information.

These men weren't here to celebrate Gregor's retirement. They were here to rob the casino. No one used this kind of weaponry for hunting. That realization galvanized her into action.

I've got to get Harris and get out of here!

She slammed the case shut and shoved it back under the bed. It didn't matter anymore if Gregor knew she'd searched his room. She planned to be as far away from here as possible when he got back.

Cally hopped up from the floor and raced downstairs to get Harris. Speeding through the kitchen, she was surprised to find it empty. Luella must have gone back to her house to rest before supper.

Collard greens simmered on the stove, their sharp scent perfuming the air. Cally could see where Luella had been slicing okra. The knife lay on the cutting board beside the dish drainer. Everything looked so normal.

She darted down the hallway to Harris's bedroom. He was still sleeping. She stopped herself from immediately snatching him up.

Think, Cally, think. What do you need to take with you?

She turned on her heel and rushed to her own room.

Keys. Car keys would be good.

She rifled through her purse searching for them. Harris was always carrying her keys around. She couldn't find them in the bag, but she knew an extra set was in her closet. She wrenched open the closet door and began hunting for the spares.

"Where are they?" she moaned out loud. She was so rattled, she could be looking straight at the keys and not seeing them.

She dug through a wicker basket of scarves and came up with a Mickey Mouse keychain.

Damn it, wrong ones. These were the keys to their old hunting cabin on the river at Palmers. They'd sold the membership and the cabin after Jamie died.

She dumped the basket on the floor and pawed through the scarves. The extra set wasn't here. *Oh, hell.* Now she remembered.

She'd been using her spares. Harris had squirreled her originals away last week, and she'd yet to find them. Maybe her current set was on the table by the back door.

She started out of the closet and remembered her gun. Standing on the bottom shelf, she had to really stretch to reach it. Her fingers closed around the grip, but she slipped off the wooden ledge, twisting her ankle.

She gritted her teeth against the pain shooting up her calf and limped to the bedroom. Shoving the gun into her purse, she hobbled to Harris's room. She tried to gently shake him awake, but he slept like a rock. If she jerked him up, he would scream bloody murder and be even more difficult to get out of the house.

"Harris, baby, wake up please." Cally tried to keep the urgency out of her voice. "Harris, honey, let's get up."

She glanced at her watch as she slowly scooped him up. This was taking too long. Gregor and his men would be back any time now.

She gathered up Harris's "blankey" and headed out. He was still dead asleep and so heavy. She'd have to get him in the car and come back for keys. She was sure they were on the chest of drawers at the back door. That's where she'd laid them when she came in from the grocery store yesterday.

The wind tore at them both as she made her way to the private entrance at the end of the hallway. The temperature was dropping, and the sky had turned a menacing green. She hurried around the side of the carport and buckled Harris into his car seat.

Miraculously, he still slept. Ignoring the pain in her ankle, she did a combination hobble and run to the back door. It was surreal to believe that just this morning she'd joked with Marcus and Harris right here about that fish.

She couldn't think about that now. *Yes!* There on the mahogany chest were her keys.

She snatched them up as the front door opened and the sound of men's voices echoed throughout the downstairs. Cally froze, barely breathing. The men came down the hallway toward the kitchen. She swallowed a groan and shoved the keys in her pocket as Gregor walked into the back foyer.

"Good afternoon, Mrs. Burnett," he said. "Are those collard greens I smell?"

Cally plastered a smile on her face and nodded, not trusting herself to speak.

"Sure smells great," Peter Sams added from behind Gregor.

Cally realized she had to say something. "Oh, it's Luella's recipe," she managed. "I know you'll enjoy it. I'll just go see if I can help her. Why don't you gentlemen have a drink in the library?"

"Sounds like a plan," said Gregor, staring at her with a curious expression.

"Dinner should be ready in…in a few minutes."

Cally turned to walk into the kitchen. She wasn't going to think about how unnatural she'd sounded. Shutting the door behind her, she scrambled across the stone floor, down the hallway and out the private entrance again. She'd almost made it around the carport when she looked across the lawn.

Luella was walking up the path toward the kitchen. Cally hesitated. She couldn't let Luella walk into the house, but she didn't have time to explain the situation. And Luella would want an explanation.

Cally glanced toward the carport. Her view of the car was blocked by a magnolia tree down the side. Cally couldn't tell if Harris was still asleep or not. She couldn't leave Luella, and the woman wasn't looking in Cally's direction.

She started to call out, but Gregor or his men might hear her. Adrenaline dulled the pain in her ankle as she darted down the path.

Luella jumped. "Oh, you gave me a start, Cally. Is something wro—"

"I don't have time to explain. You've got to get in the car and come with me right now."

Luella started to speak, but the words died on her lips when she saw Cally's eyes and the sheen of perspiration on her pale face. The older woman just nodded and started across the lawn toward the carport.

"Where's Bay?" Cally asked, taking Luella's arm to hurry her along.

"I sent him to the store for some more milk. I used it all when I was making the batter for the okra. He's not back yet."

"It's okay. We'll find him later. But we've got to get out of here. Now."

She was practically dragging Luella by the time they got to the car. Cally reached to open the door, looked inside and her blood ran cold. Harris was gone.

Chapter Seven

The wind picked up as thunder sounded in the distance. Cally swung away from the car looking wildly around her. "Harris?! Harris, where are you?"

His car seat was gone, but the blanket was still there. Her mind couldn't seem to process what her eyes were telling her as she scanned the yard, the car again, then the surrounding area once more.

"Harris! Harris, baby, answer me!"

The clouds were moving in quickly and flashes of lightning zigzagged across the sky.

"Did you lose something, Mrs. Burnett?"

Cally whirled around at the sound of Gregor's voice and stood, momentarily speechless, by the side of the car. Her mouth went dry; fear left a strong metallic taste.

"Where is he? What have you done with him, you son of a bitch?"

"Oh, Mrs. Burnett, that's no way for a Southern lady to talk." His voice dripped with sarcasm. "I'll excuse you under the circumstances. Stress can bring out the worst in people." Gregor smiled coolly. "Of course, for others it can bring out the best. At least, I've found that to be the case."

"I don't give a damn what you've found. Where's my son?"

"Oh, he's quite safe I assure you. Frank's going to take him for a little ride. You'll get him back when we're done here."

"What do you mean?"

"When we've finished our business here, you'll get Harris back all safe and sound. He'll just stay with Frank as a guarantee that you won't be tempted to tell anyone about what you found in my room."

Cally felt the rising panic claw at her chest. This wasn't happening. She heard a car door slamming and started toward the sound.

Gregor stepped in front of her, and she wouldn't have stopped—nothing would have stopped her from getting her son—except the gun in his hand pointed at her heart. She froze.

"I wouldn't do that, Mrs. Burnett. By the way, I'm surprised at you." Gregor's voice held the tone of a disapproving parent.

"Snooping around in a guest's room. I never would have thought it of you. That sense of privacy and decorum was part of my reason for picking River Trace."

More thunder boomed. The storm drew closer.

"It…was an accident." Fear for Harris and for herself made her stammer. "The brandy spilled…I never meant to look in the drawer. I was just trying to clean it…I—"

"No excuses, Mrs. Burnett. It really doesn't become you. Never apologize. That's my personal philosophy."

"Please, I won't tell anyone about what you're doing. Just, please don't hurt Harris." She felt her control slipping over the edge of the abyss. *This isn't happening. This isn't happening.* The sound of a car's tires crunching on gravel twisted her heart. They were taking her baby away from her. She swallowed and stumbled toward the drive. Gregor waved the gun at her and shook his head. Luella grabbed her arm.

"Mrs. Burnett, we won't hurt him. As long as you keep your mouth shut, he'll be just fine. You'll have him back safe and sound no later than Tuesday evening. However, if you try to contact the police or interfere in any way…" His voice trailed into the gusting wind.

Oh, God I can't do this. Her composure completely disintegrated. "No, please no. Don't do this." She clutched Gregor's arm. "I'll do anything. Please, I won't tell anyone. Just, please give him back to me."

Gregor shook his head. "Harris stays with us until this is over. When we're safely away we'll tell you where to find him."

"But why?" She was crying and her nose was running. She'd never cried pretty, and she wasn't doing it now, either, but she didn't care. "Why are you doing this?"

"For the money, of course. Do you realize what that casino makes on a holiday weekend?"

She shook her head. Still not tracking with what was happening.

"Around twelve million. Dollars. And they don't make a drop deposit until Tuesday morning. Banks are closed over Memorial Day."

"But your career…your company."

"My company." Gregor laughed—a deep, ugly, rasping sound. Cally's stomach cramped. His laughter died away; she heard more tires crunching gravel. Were they back? Maybe they weren't taking him after all? She felt a tiny flicker of hope. Gregor seemed oblivious.

"My company is about to go belly-up. There are several people who think we should go to jail."

The bitterness in Gregor's voice was palpable. He was no longer speaking to her. He was ranting.

"You know what we do, right?"

She shook her head.

"We're military contractors in Iraq. Storm's Edge." He stopped and let the name sink in.

"Oh my God." Storm's Edge had been all over the national news the past week. Even Cally had heard of them.

"Yes, *that* Storm's Edge. The one that's under judicial investigation right now." Gregor snorted and shook his head.

"I broke too many asinine administrative rules with my men in Iraq. But I got the job done when no one else could or would. I've stepped on a lot of bureaucratic toes in the process. Like it's always been, you try to help win 'em a war and the paper-pushers kick you out on your ass.

"Oh, they're using a lot of technical terms to sugarcoat it, but what it boils down to is this—after all the crap I've been through, they were actually going to try me in a criminal court. So I'm going to need the money, a lot of it, for starting a new life, somewhere else. And robbing the Paddlewheel is a fairly painless way to get it."

Cally listened in shocked silence. This was happening to someone else. She smelled rain on the air and felt the wind blowing grit—stinging her face and arms. She grimaced at the word *painless* and came back to the present.

"Why are they bringing criminal charges against you personally?"

At first she didn't think he would answer. He seemed to be staring straight through her.

"There was another matter. Let's just call it…a female problem." He laughed, a cruel rasping sound.

She shivered and spoke to cover it up. "But you're planning to hurt people. Using explosives. Guns."

"Well, since the security guards don't use them, the Paddlewheel was the natural choice." Gregor shrugged. "Don't worry. If all goes as planned, no one should get hurt, just a few explosions to distract everyone."

"You really think you can get away with it?" She looked down at the wind-tossed dandelions between her feet because she realized the answer before she'd finished asking the question.

McCay County's five deputies would be no match for these highly trained men.

There'd been several articles in the paper calling for the hire of more police to handle all the new problems the casinos had brought, but budget cuts and such being what they were—nothing had been done. Gregor's men from Storm's Edge would be more than capable of handling the local law-enforcement officials.

He didn't answer her. He didn't have to.

Lightning flashed across the sky like a scene from some kind of science-fiction movie.

It's dangerous to be standing out here in the middle of a storm. That inane thought struck as the thunder washed over them. She felt a manic giggle start to burst forth and gulped it down. The sound came out as a gasp.

She looked up to see Marcus walking toward them across the lawn. For a moment she was worried they would hurt him. Her concern changed to confusion when Gregor finally spoke. "We have everything we need to make it work."

Marcus never took his eyes from hers as he stood beside Williams. "What's going on, Gregor?"

"Oh, just explaining the facts of life to Mrs. Burnett."

Her eyes widened as the realization dawned. "Oh my God," she whispered. "You're involved in this, too?"

Marcus's jaw tightened. He looked straight through her, speaking quietly to Williams. She couldn't hear what was being said over the sounds of the growing storm.

She looked down again to see that the wind had finished ripping the heads off the dandelions. She just might be losing her mind.

Of course Marcus was involved. A security guard, or better yet, a bodyguard would be the man to know if you were planning on robbing a casino. He'd know every conceivable way in and out of the Paddlewheel. He was probably the one who'd provided those blueprints she'd found in the desk.

"Yes, Mrs. Burnett, we have a plan that covers all the contingencies. You see, we needed a man on the inside to help us, and Marcus was more than happy to assist. He's been having a few financial problems himself. And now I know we can count on your help, as well."

She stared at them both as the horror grew. "You want me to *help* you?" she asked.

"It may not be necessary. But we know you'll want to do everything possible to see that we are successful. Remember, you want us to succeed. Because if we don't, you'll never see your son alive again."

She started to protest, but nodded numbly in defeat. She'd do whatever they asked if it meant saving Harris. Thunder rolled across the sky as lightning flashed again—very close by. Rain splattered the driveway in large hard drops.

"Let's go inside. We can finish this after dinner." Gregor's tone had returned to that of the concerned parent.

She stared at him blankly. "Dinner?" she mumbled.

"We'll have dinner as planned. Those were collards I smelled earlier, yes? Can you have everything ready in thirty minutes?"

He didn't wait for her reply. She watched him walk across the beheaded dandelion stalks, talking with Marcus. Her world had just been blown to bits like the fragile weeds.

The rain began falling in earnest, but she was unaware of it until Luella tugged on her arm. Her friend had stood beside her the entire time without saying a word.

"Come on, honey. Let's get inside."

Cally didn't respond. She simply limped through the pouring rain as Luella led her back to the house.

"WHAT THE HELL were you thinking, Gregor? Kidnapping was never part of the deal!"

Marcus had been in Gregor's room along with Johnson and Sams for half an hour, discussing this new wrinkle in the program. He was not at all sure that he was handling it correctly, but acting the indignant partner left out of the loop seemed appropriate.

He couldn't believe Gregor had taken Harris.

"Keep your voice down." Gregor lounged in the easy chair warming a glass of brandy, but the look in his eyes belied his pose.

Marcus's glass sat untouched by the decanter.

"There's no reason to be concerned about the boy. This will have no effect on the plan. Everything will go on as we've discussed." Gregor took another sip of the cordial.

"What do you mean it will have no effect on the plan? It changes the plan entirely." Marcus's outrage wasn't difficult to portray.

This annihilated his strategy to call the task force in before the robbery. There was no safe way to do that now.

He wouldn't take the chance with Harris's life; that some bureaucrat might mess it up. Images of his shooting six months ago flashed across his mind.

"Kidnapping will bring the feds into it immediately. This is not what we had discussed. The risks you are taking…"

"You're damn right. It's the risk *I'm* taking." Gregor sat up straight in his chair. "You have nothing to do with this part of the undertaking. You aren't at risk until we walk through the door of the Paddlewheel."

Marcus leaned forward until he was practically nose-to-nose with Gregor. "You don't walk through the damn door of the 'Wheel without me, so that's horseshit and you know it. Kidnapping is not just an addition to the plan—it screws the plan completely."

Marcus stood and crossed to the large window at the end of the room to keep from punching Gregor in the face. His anger was genuine. Playing the role of a man trying to calm his own emotions was not a challenge. The thought of Harris being hurt made his chest ache. He'd have to examine where that came from later.

Gregor leaned back in his seat and took another sip of peach brandy. "Marcus, you don't sound like the man I hired to do the job. These are not problems to concern yourself with unless…" he let the moment hang "…you've got a new girlfriend?"

Marcus mentally grimaced as Gregor waited expectantly.

"Hell, no. It's just that the beauty of this whole idea was the simplicity. You keep adding shit, we're gonna get caught."

"I was quite specific about what would be required. At the time you told me you were willing to do and I quote, 'whatever it takes.' Well, this is what it takes. You're going to have to live with it."

"Whether this family lives or not. Right, Gregor?"

"That remains to be seen." Gregor leaned forward and picked up the decanter to pour himself another drink. "If they become a threat they will have to be eliminated."

This was what Marcus had suspected, ever since Cally had answered the door that first night. Gregor wouldn't hesitate to kill the Burnetts and the Wigginses, too—if they interfered. He had to figure out how to protect them and find the boy before he called his superiors in Jackson.

Gregor continued, "I understand you're angry. We made an executive decision without you. It couldn't be helped. The question is, are you willing to go forward?"

Gregor cut his eyes toward Sams and Johnson. Marcus knew that look and what his answer had to be. If he hesitated, he would become a threat to Gregor's plan, as well. So Marcus gave the only answer he could under the circumstances.

"Of course I am. Just don't leave me out of the damn loop anymore. It pisses me off."

Chapter Eight

Cally rocked back and forth in the darkened nursery. The only sound besides the hypnotic rain was the creak of her chair on the wooden floor. There was a nightlight shaped like a cowboy on the antique dresser. Marcus could see her clutching a small blanket to her chest as she rocked.

He stood inside the door watching her, wondering what in the hell he was doing here. She wouldn't want to see him. She'd be furious with him.

But he'd heard her weeping on the damn monitor, and he hadn't been able to stay away. He had it in his hand now. He was tired of eavesdropping—last night it was her lullaby, tonight it was her grief.

He wanted to tell her it would be okay—that he would find Harris. But he knew he couldn't tell her a thing.

So why was he standing here? Damned if he knew.

"Cally?"

She looked up in surprise. Her tears glistened in the light from the dresser.

"What do you want?" she whispered.

"I don't know," he answered honestly. "I heard you on the monitor and I couldn't…I wanted to see how you were."

He watched the emotions play across her face—shock, disbelief, anger. She didn't say anything for a moment; she just rocked as rain continued to beat on the windows.

"You're involved in this." Her voice was like ice as she rose and walked across the room to stand in front of him, meeting his gaze with arctic fury in her eyes. "And you want to know…how I am?" She enunciated the words carefully, but her tone rose at the end.

When he nodded, she slapped him. He'd known it was coming, but he made no move to stop her. The sound echoed in the room.

"You bastard," she hissed. "You fished with him this morning for God's sake." She pummeled his chest with her fists.

"Damn you! How could you do that? How could you?" She shouted as tears streamed down her face like a river.

There was nothing he could do to help her, so he let her hit him and rage. He didn't try to stop her hands until she clawed at him, then he held her wrists.

"He's all alone with them because I…I left him in that car. He's…he's afraid of the dark and he has nightmares. He doesn't have his blanket and he can't…he can't sleep without it. Do…do you think they know that?"

He looked into her tear-filled eyes. Her nose was running. Her long red hair had come loose from its braid; her breath came in deep gasps.

She stared back at him a moment before he pulled her toward him. He was surprised she wasn't kneeing him in the groin. He kissed the top of her head and held her to him as she wept. She needed the comfort of someone to hang on to as she cried. Even he would do. She was too wrecked emotionally to stop him. Besides that, what more could he do for her? Tell her the truth?

Hell, if he did she might use it to bargain with Gregor—thinking it would save Harris. Telling her the truth would only put them both in more danger. He couldn't take that chance. He would find Harris before the robbery, but until he had the child safely back, there was nothing to say.

She thinks I'm a monster. He'd known this was coming, but it still burned like acid.

He pulled away, put the monitor in her hands and turned to walk out of the room. He was almost to the door when he heard her now-quiet voice.

"Why did you do it?"

He turned back to her. "What?"

"Why did you make friends with us? The fishing this morning, the coffee last night? What are you doing here right now?"

He stood, locked into her stare. God, the answer to that would scare them both to death, and she was in no condition for what he was really doing there. What he'd wanted to do the first time she'd answered the door in that transparent blouse.

Finally, he dropped his eyes—frightened of what she would see there.

Cally continued. "If you knew what was going to happen when you got here, why did you act like you cared?"

"It wasn't an act." He looked up again to meet her questioning eyes, and this time he let the heat blast her. He couldn't believe he'd said those words out loud.

What am I doing? Get out of here now, North, before you make a complete ass of yourself.

Cally stared at him with the monitor in her hands and disbelief written all over her face. Then something in her eyes changed. And he should have cared, should have stopped to figure out what it was, but she was stepping toward him and wrapping herself around him and unbelievably she was kissing the hell out of him. Practically climbing up his chest.

The monitor clattered to the ground as her hips knocked into his and her breasts pressed into his chest. His body responded and his mind disconnected from everything except how incredible she felt.

She pushed harder against him and sucked his bottom lip into her mouth. Her arms reached up to circle his neck, pulling him down closer. Then her tongue was sweeping into his mouth, and he was well and truly lost.

His hands slipped around her waist, and he lifted her up so that they were more evenly matched in height. There was no place to go but the wall, so he braced her back there and held her butt as she tugged at his jeans' zipper. He unbuttoned her shirt.

She had a hand in his boxers and he was leaning his head back, one hand halfway under her bra, when he pulled back to look at her face. That's when he saw her eyes.

Ice-blue. Hard and staring at the crib over his shoulder.

She was a million miles away, one lone tear streaking down her cheek.

He froze and when she turned her frigid gaze on him, it was all he could do to hang on to her.

"What is it, Marcus?"

He could hear the tinge of desperation in her voice as she tightened her legs around his waist. His body responded and he knew he was a dog for not pulling away, even as he was trying to figure out how to salvage the situation.

"I'll blow your mind six ways to Sunday. I'll do everyone in Gregor's group, too, if you'll give me back my son. Is this what it's going to take?" Her voice was barely a whisper, but it stirred the air by his ear.

He shook his head, struggling to hang on to her; he was so shaken by what was happening. He was more aroused than he'd been in a very long time, and this was so *not* going to happen. They both knew it.

"That's not. God, Cally, that's not what this is about."

Good Lord. Of course that's what she thought this was about. He was doing his job very, very well.

"What, did you think I wasn't capable of this? I'll do anything you want if you'll just, please…" her voice hitched "…give…him back to me."

She broke again, completely. Weeping and wrapped in his

arms. They were still braced against the nursery wall; she laid her head on his shoulder.

He lowered her to the floor, gently buttoning her blouse and zipping his jeans. Leading her back to the rocker where he'd found her earlier, he sat her down and pulled a small blanket off the loveseat to tuck around her. She looked like a broken china doll.

His heart broke for the hell she was going through. For what he, in own idiocy, had just put her through. Rain beat against the roof. He had to leave now, before he told her everything— who he really was, what he was really doing here.

Because she'd tell Gregor. She'd just proven that where Harris was concerned, she'd do absolutely anything and she'd do it extraordinarily well, to get her son back.

MARCUS TOOK a detour through the paneled library before he went back up to his attic room. He was going to have a drink, *damn it,* and a cold shower. He picked up a crystal glass and poured himself a shot.

Instead of one, he had two. He could still see Cally's face, hear the devastation in her words. He shook his head trying to clear the images. Then he decided "to hell with it," tucked the bottle under his arm and started back up the steps.

He was thinking about Cally and Harris—not looking where he was going. He'd just made the first landing when he tripped. He'd never know why—whether it was the liquor or clumsiness— but he ended up flat on his face. The bottle somehow didn't break.

He lay there for a moment—stunned, panicked, then positively furious. What the hell was he doing?

I promised myself I'd never be here again.

He jerked himself up and stalked back down to the kitchen. So angry at himself, his hand shook as he poured the contents of Cally's bottle of ten-year-old Scotch down the drain.

He'd replace her liquor later.

For now, he'd worked too hard to beat this after Tessa died. He'd sworn he'd never get that out of control again. Besides, Hodges would have a cow.

"Hi. My name is Marcus. I'm an alcoholic undercover police officer."

It'd almost be worth it to see the look on the lieutenant's face.

RAIN PELTED the windshield as Peter Sams and Rob Johnson pulled off the county highway beside an abandoned cotton field. A mattress factory, closed for the weekend, was a few hundred yards farther up the road. They jogged the rest of the way in.

The explosives in their backpacks weren't heavy. Magnesium pencil flares weighed less than two and a half ounces apiece. Lightweight mechanical alarm clocks served as timers. They set four flares each in various parts of the plant. Mattress World Corporation had a sprinkler system, but the antiquated fire alarm would be no match for eight flares igniting several hundred yards of cotton batting.

One night watchman was asleep in his truck around the side of the building. He never knew they were there. In total, it took fifteen minutes to break in, set the devices and get out. Sams and Johnson were at the bridge on River Road forty minutes later.

The rain had stopped but the wind picked up considerably. Sams pulled to the shoulder and Johnson took a car jack out of the trunk. To any passerby they appeared to be changing a flat, but the ruse wasn't necessary.

Only two cars passed and no one could see Johnson climbing down the side of the culvert as Sams set the C-4 charges at either end of the bridge.

"The auxiliaries are in place," called Sams. "And you lost the toss."

"Yeah, I know. I'm on my way to take care of it," mumbled Johnson, going over the mental list in his head. *C-4, detonators, wire, transmi—*

The tall grass rustled and fear slithered down his back as he lost track of the list. He hoped he didn't come across any snakes in this underbrush. He hated snakes. Poisonous or not, he hated them.

He shook his head to clear away the nerves. He didn't like thinking about potential problems. He was twenty-four hours from an incredible new future.

He crawled down into the ditch, and slogged through the decayed-smelling mud to set the timers and explosives on top of the conduit under the bridge. The metal tubing was small, clearly marked with the local phone company's logo. It held all the landline phone cables leading from the casino to the cell tower a half mile away.

The bridge spanned only fifty feet—not a very noble structure, but when disabled, there would be no outside communications available to the Paddlewheel and the only access would be the Mississippi River.

Chapter Nine

Monday morning

Marcus trotted up the steps to the old store's porch. He had jogged in from River Trace to this specific place to make a phone call. There was no way he was having this conversation at the bed-and-breakfast on his cell. Boggs had too many scanners and Marcus's phone, while high-tech, was operating in analog mode out here in the sticks. Everything was too easily monitored.

Old-school was the only way to go. It wasn't foolproof, but it was far safer than using his cell for now. Still, he wished the pay phone was inside. He felt exposed standing on the front porch of the bait shop.

He hoped Asa was home. He didn't know who else to call if he wasn't.

An elderly man behind the counter sold Marcus a quart of Gatorade. He downed half the bottle on his way back outside. He dialed and listened as the phone rang several times before being picked up.

He smiled as he heard a crash and a muffled, "Damn it." Asa cleared his throat. "Yeah, I'm here. This better be good." He had a deep smoker's voice that sounded like a metal door opening on a rusty hinge.

"You're so pleasant first thing in the morning."

"Christ of mercy, Marcus, what time is it?"

"A little after six. Rise and shine, big guy."

"Go to hell."

Marcus evaluated last night. "I've done that already. Thanks just the same. How's Trey?"

Asa's voice dropped, "No real change. The doctors say it's going to take some more time."

And a hell of a lot more money, thought Marcus, but he didn't say that out loud.

Asa's sixteen-year-old son was in a rehabilitation center outside Jackson, recovering from a serious car wreck last summer. Learning to walk again was incredibly expensive. Insurance paid part of the bill, but not all.

There was a long pause and Marcus had the uncomfortable feeling that Asa had read his mind.

"What's up, besides me?" Asa rumbled.

"Well...I need some help, partner."

"Lord, don't say that too loud. Hodges might have apoplexy. You of all people know how dangerous I am to your career. I believe it's called professional leprosy."

Marcus snorted. "Yeah. Well, screw Hodges."

Asa's deep booming laugh crackled over the phone line. "Actually I'm not that kind of guy. But I'll help with anything else I can. Internal Affairs has been breathing down my neck and Hodges has been waiting for your call. When's the job going down?"

"Tonight."

"Tonight? Have you told Hodges?"

"No, not exactly." Marcus felt like the child caught with his hand in the proverbial cookie jar. "There's a complication I'm not sure how to handle."

"What kind of complication?" There was no levity in Asa's voice now.

Marcus explained about Harris and listened to the silence.

Finally Asa spoke. "You think the boy's still alive?"

"Yeah, I do, right now. I just don't know for how long. If this thing starts to unravel, I don't trust Gregor to stay cool. I've got to find Harris before I call Hodges."

"Do you think that's the wisest choice?"

Why had he asked that?

"Hell, no. This worries me on so many levels. I mean, God, the last time I was involved in an undercover bust, I got shot."

"I know," Asa's voice was quiet.

Marcus mentally kicked himself. They had yet to talk about what had happened that night, except to agree that Marcus had been judged guilty by association and Asa felt horrible about it. They needed to talk, but now was not the time. "I'm also worried about a leak."

"What do you mean...a leak?" asked Asa.

"Once I contact the task force, different divisions will become involved. All that radio traffic worries me. One of Gregor's men is a technological guru with access to all kinds of police scanners and such. With all the different agencies and communications traffic involved in a multi-jurisdictional deal like this one, those wires will be lit up like a Christmas tree."

"Hmm. And, of course, there's always the possibility our efficient command could screw up the bust," added Asa.

Marcus laughed under his breath and rubbed his injured shoulder. "It's been known to happen. And if it does, I think Harris and his mother will be the ones to pay. My concern is that Gregor will slip through the cracks during all this confusion and I don't—"

"So what do you want me to do?" interrupted Asa.

"Come help me. Unofficially, of course."

"Oh, of course."

Marcus knew what he was asking. With the Internal Affairs investigation in full swing, they'd have Asa's hide if they knew he was anywhere close to the operation at the Paddlewheel. But their friendship overrode that practical consideration. Asa would walk through fire to help Marcus, no questions asked. Marcus knew that was true because he'd been walking through an inferno himself since the raid last November.

"You sure about this, Marcus? I mean—the department's lightning efficiency aside."

Marcus snorted at the comment.

"If you play this by the book, it could go a long way toward clearing up the mess that being associated with me has made of your career," Asa continued. "They could arrest Gregor and his crew in the act and you'll come home a hero. Not to mention, it'll make Hodges look like the horse's ass we both know he is for trying to pull you off the governor's task force along with me."

Marcus thought for a minute—of all the things that were unsaid, of Hodges and his own "short leash" since Asa's suspension. There just wasn't time to go there right now. "Yeah, partner. I'm sure. If this thing gets screwed up because of the bureaucracy there in Jackson and something happens to that boy, I'll feel responsible."

"Is it just the kid you feel responsible for or something else?"

Actually—it was *someone* else, but Marcus didn't voice that thought, either. "I'm not sure." Marcus was lying and Asa probably knew it, but that was okay. Sometimes partners were good for letting you lie to yourself and to them, too. Because Marcus *was* sure. He felt responsible for both Harris and Cally.

When did that happen? When had he let it happen? Well, that was pretty easy to figure out. When he'd had Cally pinned against the nursery wall, his hands on her ass and his tongue down her throat.

Never mind that she wasn't exactly "feeling it" the same for him. This was all too emotionally frightening to dwell on, and he definitely wasn't going there right now with his partner. He needed a session with Dr. Phil or more likely Jerry Springer to figure things out.

"All right, Marcus. Tell me what to do."

They talked for a few more minutes and, when he hung up the pay phone, Marcus had a plan. It wasn't completely ironed out, but it was a start. He trotted down the store's porch stairs with Asa's parting words echoing in his head.

Be careful, and if you change your mind about calling Hodges in, remember. He's an ass, but a competent one. If anybody can keep the lid on this thing, it's him.

Marcus wasn't sure whether he was making the right decision or not. There just weren't many good options here.

He stretched and checked his watch. Time had gotten away from him, and he still had a twenty-minute jog ahead.

THE AROMA of brewing coffee wafted into the nursery, slowly waking Cally. She stretched and tried to get comfortable, a difficult proposition due to the large hump under her left shoulder.

Keeping her eyes closed, she enjoyed the sensation of being on the edge of sleep. *Hmm, Luella must be fixing breakfast. I'll get Harris up in a minute and go help her.*

Cally stretched again before bolting upright on the loveseat. The events of last night came rushing back with gut-wrenching clarity. She was in the nursery, but Harris wasn't here.

I left him in the car, and they took him.

The shock and emptiness had an immediate chilling effect on her stomach. Her head ached; her eyes felt gritty. She wasn't sure how long she'd slept. Perhaps two hours.

Everything felt heavy—as though she was moving underwater. She reached down to pull the stuffed elephant she had accidentally slept on into her lap. Wrapping her arms around the gray plush pachyderm, the sharp, hot tears surprised her. She hadn't thought she could have any left after last night.

Oh, God. Harris was out there all alone. Was he frightened? Was he still alive?

Yes, he had to be. She wasn't going to even think otherwise.

But, oh, he must be so scared. Wondering what had happened to his little world. Wondering where his Momma was.

She felt the scalding tears on her cheeks again. *I've got to stop this. I won't be any help to Harris if I'm a basket case.*

She remembered what Gregor had told her and Luella last night after dinner. He had spoken like he was issuing orders to his men.

"Everything continues as normal or the child dies. Breakfast will be at 9:00 a.m., lunch at 12:30 p.m. and dinner at 9:00 p.m. You and the Wigginses are not to use a house or cell phone or leave the premises. If anyone stops by for a visit, get rid of them as quickly as possible. If they ask about Harris's whereabouts, tell them he is sleeping."

He assured her that if she followed his instructions, she would have Harris back no later than Tuesday afternoon. He'd made no more mention of her helping with the actual robbery.

How in the world could she have helped, anyway? She surprised herself with the answer. Very easily if it meant saving Harris.

She would do whatever she was asked in order to get Harris back safe and sound—she would even kill. The clarity with which that thought came stunned her. She had never thought of herself as a violent person, but after last night with Marcus, she knew she was capable of anything where her child's safety was concerned. She figured most people felt the same way about their children. Cally had just never been put to the test till now.

Please, Harris. Baby, just hang on until Tuesday. The tears came faster now. She had to stop crying.

This was what it had been like when Jamie died. She hadn't been able to control the grief. It had frightened her how the emotions could turn from sorrow to fury in mere seconds.

She thought about how far she'd been willing to take the charade with Marcus. There'd been a moment when she'd thought she was going to have sex with him. She'd gladly have done it to get Harris back. She'd surprised herself at how willing she'd been to let that boundary fall away. But Marcus had stopped her. Why?

He had certainly been playing a part since he'd walked through the door of River Trace. She could have sworn she'd seen regret and something else she hadn't wanted to acknowledge before he left the nursery. The look in his eyes had touched her. Unfortunately, it was all pretense. It had to be. What other explanation was there?

She'd been taken in by the whole bunch. Lord, she'd even thought Gregor was a nice guy the last time he'd stayed at her bed-and-breakfast. Her judgment in people, especially men, was severely lacking.

She swiped angrily at the salty drops running down her cheeks and rose from the small sofa. In the empty kitchen she poured herself a cup of coffee, added cream and sugar, then sat listlessly holding the steaming cup without taking one sip. Instead, she looked out toward the lake.

She desperately wanted to call the police, but Gregor's threats of what he would do to Harris if he caught her were frightening. Could she risk it? She didn't know where the men were right now.

Sams or Johnson could be anywhere. Maybe if she looked upstairs in their rooms, she could find their cell phones? Frozen by indecision, she was loath to do anything that would put her son in more danger.

Mist hung over the water like a ghostly shroud. Ducks paddled at the end of the dock—foraging. The atmosphere was calm and deceptively tranquil. As she watched one of the ducks, Marcus strolled onto the dock.

She started to turn away. Now was the time she could look in his room for a phone. But curiosity kept her rooted to the spot.

Her eyes filled once more when he sat in the same place he had yesterday with Harris. She was torturing herself, but she couldn't stop staring. His shoulders slumped as he looked out across the lake.

What was he doing out there?

She drew closer to the window. Her tears dried and suddenly the anger was just…there. Full-force, no warning. Before she realized what she was doing, she was headed down the hallway and out the back door—coffee cup in hand.

Chapter Ten

Marcus stared out over the mist-shrouded water, replaying yesterday morning with Bay and Harris in his head. He did not have time to be out here. He should be inside with Gregor. But he didn't want to slip back into that charade yet.

The peacefulness he'd felt yesterday was gone. God, this had become a Gordian knot.

The smart thing to do would be to contact Hodges. Just call in the cavalry. Marcus would get back into the department's good graces and they'd find Harris...or get the child killed.

That, of course, was the stumbling block to the whole idea. He just couldn't bring himself to trust the bureaucracy in Jackson to handle this without fumbling.

Hodges was good at his job. Marcus didn't like him, but he did trust him. It was all the other people involved that had him worried.

Then there was Cally Burnett. How was he going to protect her from Gregor? The man would kill her if necessary to expedite the plan.

Marcus hadn't known she existed forty-eight hours ago, yet now he was considering risking what was left of his career and, quite possibly, his life, to help her and her son.

When had she gotten under his skin?

Pretty much the moment she'd opened the door to River Trace Saturday night.

That wasn't her fault, he just liked her too much. All his resolutions to keep everything strictly professional had been seriously strained from the beginning.

Sitting with her that first night and talking while she rocked her child. She'd made him think things and want things he hadn't wanted since…ever.

That longing for peace he'd been struggling with had come into focus when he'd sat drinking coffee with her in the moonlight—that yearning for something clean and good. He'd forgotten those things existed until he'd met her. He cared what she thought of him.

And then there was Harris. When that boy reached for Marcus's hand on the pier Sunday morning, Cally's son had grabbed ahold of his heart, as well. Marcus had to find him.

He turned from the water and his pity party when he heard footsteps. Cally marched across the broad cypress planks holding a cup of coffee.

He was momentarily stunned as if in thinking of the woman, he'd conjured her from thin air. She stopped in front of him with molten fury in her eyes.

"Good morning," Marcus said, recovering his speech. "I don't suppose that coffee's for me, is it?"

His attempt at humor fell flat. She ignored his greeting, and he watched as she slowly pulled her teeth across her plump lower lip. A rather erotic-looking gesture, though he knew that was definitely not her intent.

"What kind of game are you playing?" she demanded. "Why did you do this?"

He was amazed at the incredible change that had come over her. Last night she'd been hysterical…broken. This morning she was dry-eyed as anger shimmered off her in waves.

"You aren't who you said you were. What did you mean about this 'not being an act?'"

Lord, he wanted to tell her who he was so badly. Just tell

her so that she'd quit looking at him as if he were something she needed to wipe off the bottom of her shoe.

His thoughts waged a war.

Just tell her.

You can't. It's too dangerous.

It's her son. She could help.

He felt himself weakening. To combat the weakness he got angry himself. "Who do you think I am? I'm the monster who helped take your son after I heard his nightmares and went fishing with him. What do you think?"

"I don't know, but you're not the same as those others. You're different. I know that."

"How do you know that? Why do you think I'm any different from Gregor and his crew? I could have been lying. How can you tell?"

"Because. I just know. I can sense it. Harris sensed it, too. When he had his nightmare, you cared. Last night when you came to check on me—" she blushed but kept on doggedly "—you told me the caring was real. Was it?"

Cally leaned in to look more closely at his face. Her hair held that same herbal scent Marcus remembered from last night. He recoiled from the memory as well as her words.

But she didn't stop talking. "I could tell in your eyes you meant that. You aren't who Gregor thinks you are. Are you?"

He was trapped and momentarily speechless. He was going to tell her who he really was any minute, and that would put them both in danger.

She'd been moving closer to him as they'd been arguing. Looking over her shoulder, he saw Gregor striding toward them across the lawn.

Williams hadn't reached the end of the pier yet; he hadn't heard what they were saying. But he was obviously curious about what was up between his bought-and-paid-for bodyguard and the unwilling host of his casino robbery gang.

Marcus had to get her to shut up about him being different, or they would both be in trouble. So he did the first thing that came to mind. What he'd wanted to do since that first night he saw her in those wet clothes. What he'd promised himself he wouldn't do again after last night's disaster in the nursery.

He grabbed Cally by the waist, pulled her to him and kissed her. He'd meant for it to be a bruising staged kiss—for Gregor's benefit, as well as their own safety. But it didn't quite turn out that way.

Oh, initially the kiss was rough, but then he gentled his lips and eased her mouth open—and found that he couldn't stop. Running his tongue around the inside of her mouth, he forgot what he was supposed to be doing.

She pushed against him with her left hand, her right still held the coffee cup crushed between their bodies. He angled his head and pulled her firmly into his hips. She was trying to crush his foot but he didn't care. He took the kiss deeper, bending her slightly back over his arm. She quit stepping on his toes.

He ran one hand up from her waist to press against the side of her breast. She murmured something unintelligible and tentatively touched his tongue with her own. His other hand went lower. She pushed against him, lifted a hand to the back of his neck and he pulled her closer. He opened his eyes to look at her as she kissed him back.

This was better than last night. This time she wasn't hysterical. She was responding with what appeared to be honesty. Then he realized he wasn't thinking at all. He was losing himself in her again.

He pulled away so quickly she fell against his chest. She looked up at him in shocked surprise. Her eyes were huge—filled with confusion and vulnerability.

What had just happened? As Marcus's vision cleared, he could see that Gregor had stopped at the end of the pier. Williams was watching their little drama unfold. Cally hadn't seen him yet but Marcus had to do something. She was about to speak when he interrupted her.

"That's who I am, Cally," Marcus's voice boomed over the quiet water. "I take what I want, when I want. Sometimes I'm charming about it, usually I'm not. But I can be very obliging. We have a little time before I have to leave. What do you say? Wanna come up to my room?"

She stared at him as he spoke, dumbfounded, and her eyes turned from soft vulnerability to a deep frigid blue. He didn't see her raise the cup until coffee was splashing over his face. He tasted the sugar and cream and heard Gregor's rasping laugh.

"Oh, you have quite a way with the ladies, Marcus."

Cally gasped and whirled around, before turning back to face Marcus with a panicked expression on her face.

"I take it that's a *no*," he said softly. "But I think you'd better leave now." He nodded toward Gregor. "*He* doesn't take *no* for an answer."

She lowered her head and hurried away, not even acknowledging Gregor as she passed.

"And good morning to you, too, Mrs. Burnett."

Marcus scraped his thoughts together as he waited for Gregor at the end of the pier. He had to get his head straight to do this. No distractions. Cally in his arms—warm, soft, kissing him back, for God's sake. *Distraction* was a mild term for what the woman had become.

"What time are you going in to work today?" Gregor asked.

"I'll be leaving in the next hour or so. I've got to get cleaned up."

"Naturally, you can't go to work with coffee grounds in your hair," said Gregor. "I'm renting a boat again today to go check on the airstrip. I want to make sure it's still above water level."

Marcus ignored the sarcasm. "So we're all set for tonight?"

"Looks like."

"I'll go get showered and touch base before I leave."

Gregor nodded. They started back to the house. Marcus was distinctly aware of the speculative looks Gregor was shooting him. *He suspects something.* Deciding the best defense was a good offense, Marcus stopped at the end of the pier and faced him.

"Is there something you want to ask me?"

There was a long pause.

"Hmm. Don't really see the need," Gregor finally replied. "You said so yourself. You never kiss and tell."

CALLY PRACTICALLY sprinted back to the house, her ankle protesting the entire way. She fidgeted with the empty coffee cup and made a conscious effort to hold it still in her hand. Her response to Marcus's kiss had been frightening. A part of her had enjoyed it—enjoyed kissing the man who had helped take Harris. What was wrong with her? She could still taste him on her lips.

Trembling with fury and thoroughly disgusted with herself, she stalked to the kitchen entrance. She wasn't going to lie to herself. Last night she'd been trying to get Harris back. Today she'd really been kissing Marcus. Was she going crazy? She slammed into the back foyer and the doorbell rang, jangling her already frayed nerves.

Who in the world?

Gregor's warning flashed into her mind. She had to get rid of whoever it was as quickly as possible. She passed through the hallway by the grand staircase and Peter Sams stared down over the top railing.

She glared back. Lord, she hoped she could do this. Taking a deep gulp of air, she conjured up a weak smile and swung the door open.

"Surprise!" Her heart sank as Kevin Tucker wrapped her in

a huge bear hug. Her dear friend was the one person she wouldn't be able to get rid of quickly.

"Kevin! What on earth are you doing here?"

"Good Lord, Cally. What kind of greeting is that? I haven't seen you in two weeks." He flashed his devastating smile.

"Oh, Kevin, I'm sorry. It's just such a shock to see you here."

"Well, I know. I'm passing through on my way to Monroe. You remember my brother. He and his wife just had a baby. Woo-hoo! I'm an uncle and about to meet my new niece."

"Congratulations. When was she born?" She felt her world spin even more out of control and asked the routine question on automatic pilot.

"Last night. She was eight pounds, five ounces."

"That's wonderful."

"I'm pretty excited about it. I guess that makes Roger an aunt."

Cally gave him a weak smile. Roger was Kevin's significant other. She'd waited tables with them both when she was working her way through college in Memphis.

"How is Roger doing? Is he still performing at the Peabody on weekends?"

"Yeah. Now that it's warmed up, his jazz combo plays on The Roof every Friday and Saturday. You'll have to come up soon for the weekend and stay with us. Bring Harris. It'll be great fun."

Cally didn't trust herself to talk, so she nodded instead.

"Speaking of Harris, where is that charmer?"

"He's napping."

Kevin wrinkled his forehead. "Awfully early for a nap."

Cally swallowed audibly. How could she get rid of Kevin? He knew her so well, and Harris, too. Well enough to know that her son didn't normally nap at nine o'clock in the morning. She didn't know what to tell him.

"Honey, what's wrong? He's not sick is he?"

She grasped onto the lifeline he'd involuntarily thrown her.

"Actually, Harris has a touch of the stomach flu. It's been rather brutal." Cally began to warm to her story. "We were awake last night till four." That part at least wasn't a lie.

"You poor thing. You must be exhausted. Is there anything I can do?" He headed toward the staircase and Harris's room.

"No, no. We'll be fine. Luella and Bay are a great help." She stopped at the bottom step, effectively barring his way—all the while twisting the coffee cup around in her hands. "Besides, I wouldn't want to expose you to this if you're going to see that precious new baby."

"Lord, if I didn't know you better I would think you were trying to get rid of me."

She gave a laugh that sounded false even to her ears. "Of course I'm not trying to get rid of you. I just don't want you to get this stomach virus."

Kevin studied her with a puzzled expression and glanced up as Peter Sams walked down the staircase.

"Hello."

Sams nodded to Kevin's greeting. "Good morning, Mrs. Burnett." He passed them on his way to the dining room.

"Morning, Mr. Sams," Cally mumbled. She stared after him as he walked into the dining room and closed the door.

Kevin watched her, his expression becoming more puzzled. "Business is good, huh?"

"Hmm?" She jerked her eyes away from the closed door. "Oh, yes, business is great."

"I won't stay long, but could I get a cup of coffee before I go?"

"Of course you can." She smiled genuinely for the first time since Kevin had arrived—relieved that he'd quit questioning her about Harris and that he would soon be leaving. "Let's go into the kitchen."

"How are the Wigginses doing?"

"They're just great. Doing real well. Don't know what I'd do without them."

"Uh-huh."

Gregor and Marcus were still out on the pier. Sams was on his way across the lawn to the dock. Did she have time to make that phone call to the police before they came back in?

She didn't know where Boggs and Johnson were. Could she risk it anyway? Could she do that and get Kevin out of here before everyone came back inside?

"Kevin, could I use your cell phone? Our phones are out of order this morning and I need to make a phone call to the pharmacy to check on some medicine for Harris." She died a little at the thought of endangering Kevin by using his phone but told herself it was for everyone's benefit.

"Of course. I can run to town and get the prescription for you if you need me to." He pulled an iPhone from his pocket. "Here you go."

"No! I mean— That won't be necessary. Bay can get it for me. He's got a list from Luella, so he'll be going to town anyway. Besides you've got to go see that new niece." She held the phone and hesitated over who to dial and how to talk with Kevin standing there.

"Okay. Um…Cally, you think Luella'll let me have that recipe for seafood gumbo this time?"

She wasn't really listening as she studied the screen and tried to look out the window at the same time. Gregor and Marcus were still outside. Sams was with them. She could do this.

"Cally?"

"Sure she will. Just ask her." She walked to the counter and poured two cups of coffee, then dialed 911. The call rang through, but she had to get out of here to talk.

"Yeah, I'll do that."

"I can give you this in a disposable cup if you like." *That way you can take it with you.* "You want some hazelnut creamer?"

"No," Kevin came to stand beside her.

She was totally focused on the phone. Why wasn't 911

picking up? "Can you excuse me a minute? I'm just going to talk to them in the other room."

"No, I can't. Cally, what in the hell is going on here? You know Luella won't give me that recipe. Over the past two years I've asked her for it half a dozen times. She says it's her family's biggest secret. It's been the running joke whenever I've come to visit you."

Cally pulled her gaze from the phone and focused on Kevin, her stomach knotting tighter as he continued to speak.

"What's wrong, sweetie?" he asked. "Everything's not okay, I can tell. You're chewing a hole through that lovely bottom lip of yours and you're calling 911."

She gasped.

"iPhones have huge screens, darling. Come on, let me help you."

She couldn't do this. She just had to get him out. Now.

"Kevin, damn it. Don't ask me any more questions." Her voice was quiet but determined. "If you really want to help me, just walk out of here. Get in your car and leave. I can't explain, but I'm begging you."

Cally turned to look out the window for Gregor and Marcus. They were gone.

"That's the one thing I won't do."

"Kevin, listen to what I'm telling you. Please. Go. Now. Before it's too late."

"Too late for what?"

God, she'd handled this all wrong.

"They're coming. Just go. Get out of here." She pulled his arm toward the kitchen door but slipped the phone in her pocket. "I can't talk now, and I need you to leave. I can't have you here. I don't want you here."

"Mrs. Burnett, that's no way to talk to a friend."

Cally froze at the sound of Gregor's voice.

"You wouldn't want him to get suspicious now, would you?"

Gregor stood in the hall's entryway leading to her bedroom. Marcus and Sams were behind him.

"Who are you?" demanded Kevin.

"No one you need to worry about. You really should have listened to Mrs. Burnett when she asked you to leave."

Gregor strolled into the kitchen. "You see, now I'm afraid it's too late for you to go anywhere."

"What's going on?" Kevin still didn't understand even when he saw the gun. "Cally?"

"No! Please don't hurt him. It's my fault." She stood in front of Kevin. "He won't tell anyone. Please."

"I told you there would be consequences if you disobeyed my orders." Gregor shook his head.

"Move, Mrs. Burnett." He raised the gun.

"No! Please, no!" She moved forward to pull on his arm.

Kevin pushed against the door with his back, both hands raised to shoulder level.

"Gregor, there's no need," said Marcus. "He can stay here with the rest of—"

The sound of the gun's blast drowned out the last of his words. Cally screamed as Kevin fell back against the door. Blood gushed over his face.

"Kevin. Oh my God, no. Kevin!" Cally rushed to him and pulled his bloodied head into her lap. His left temple was gashed. She pressed her shaking hands against the side of his face in an attempt to stop the bleeding. His blood was warm and tacky against her palms.

Marcus grabbed two towels from the counter and bent down to help her. Kevin was unconscious but still breathing. "Good Christ, Gregor. Was that really necessary?" Marcus demanded.

"That was a warning shot. The next time you try to dictate my behavior, I'll shoot to kill. I may need *you* to get into the casino, but others—" he looked pointedly at Cally "—are more disposable." Having made his point, he stepped over Kevin to leave the kitchen. Sams followed him out the door.

Marcus knelt down and pressed the cloth to the wound.

The coppery scent of blood mingled in the air with the odor of gunpowder. The surreal aspect of it all was keeping Cally calm for the moment. She inhaled through her mouth to avoid the smell.

"How bad is it?" she asked softly.

"I'm not sure. Looks like it grazed his temple."

"Will he be okay?"

He looked at her bloodstained hands before answering, "I don't know. Head wounds are tricky. They bleed like crazy. Let's get him off the floor and see if we can stop the bleeding."

She stood to try and help carry Kevin.

"I can't lift him, he's too heavy."

"Go find Bay. He can do it."

"That's right. Bay was a hospital corpsman in Korea, too. He'll know how to help. I'll be right back."

She didn't have to look far. Bay and Luella were rushing up from the guest cottage when she stepped outside. They'd heard the gunshot.

"What happened to you?" shouted Bay.

Cally realized she was covered in blood. "It's not mine. I'm all right, but we need your help. Gregor shot Kevin." They raced up the back steps to the side entrance.

"When did Kevin get… Oh, that's not important. Where's he at?" asked Luella.

"He's in the kitchen. Marcus is with him now."

Luella and Bay stopped for a moment and looked questioningly at her.

"I don't know what's going on," she said. "Marcus is trying to help Kevin. That's all that matters right now."

Without another word they followed her inside.

"Where do you want to take him?" asked Marcus.

"My room," said Cally.

Marcus held Kevin's head and Bay held his feet as they carried him down the hall and eased him onto the elaborate four-poster bed that had once belonged to Jamie's grandmother.

After last night Cally wouldn't have believed it possible, but in the past ten minutes her nightmare had intensified. She grabbed several towels from the bathroom along with hydrogen peroxide.

Bay had the experience here so everyone began taking orders from him. He sent Luella to find scissors and boil them. Marcus stayed to help with cleaning the wound. Cally followed Luella down the hall as far as the nursery.

Once there she quietly shut the door and pulled out Kevin's cell phone. It was covered in blood. She grabbed a handful of baby wipes to clean it and taking a deep breath, she stared at the screen before dialing.

This could be their one chance. She dialed 911. She hit Send. Nothing happened.

The call wouldn't go through. She tried again.

Damn it. Coverage out here could be bad, but never like this.

The knock on the door had her fumbling and almost dropping the phone.

"Cally? You okay? I need some help finding rubbing alcohol." Marcus opened the door without hesitating and caught her with the phone in her hands.

"What are you doing?" he asked

"I'm trying to get help."

He saw the 911 on the screen. "Have you talked to anyone yet?"

The call was finally going through and ringing. "911. What is your emergency?"

"Hang it up," demanded Marcus.

"But Kevin—"

"Hang it up *now*, Cally. Gregor has scanners that can pick up that call. He'll know exactly who you talked to and what you said. The police won't be able to get here fast enough to save any of you once he knows you've contacted the authorities."

"What is the nature of your emergency?"

Cally stared at the phone then looked up at Marcus. He had every reason to lie but it seemed as if he was most worried about her getting hurt. He could easily take the phone from her. Why wasn't he?

"What is the nature of your emergency?"

"Why should I believe you?"

"I can't think of one good reason."

She hit End. "Who the hell are you?"

"The monster who helped take your son, and who is trying to save your friend. Remember that. Now, I need your help with Kevin. Are you coming?"

She looked around the nursery and beat back despair as she nodded. Was she a fool to trust Marcus or had she just saved their lives by not calling 911?

"Give me the phone." He held out his hand. She slapped it into his palm and followed him down the hall.

Bay was cleaning Kevin's wound. It was oval-shaped and jagged around the edges but not terribly deep. A flap of skin the size of a quarter hung at the hairline. She washed up and handed Bay everything he asked for.

She wasn't sure how much blood Kevin had lost, but he was deathly pale. Luella returned with the sterilized scissors and went back in search of more linens for bandages.

Bay was worried about his hands. "I'm eighty-three and just not as steady as I need to be here. But I can tell you what to do."

Marcus nodded. Cally held Kevin's head while he trimmed the blond hair away from his temple.

"He needs a doctor," she said.

"Gregor will never allow that."

"I know, but he needs stitches."

"So we'll have to take care of him ourselves—Bay can tell us what to do."

She tried to wipe away the blood on Kevin's cheek and glare at Marcus at the same time.

"I can help, if you'll let me, Cally."

"Of course, I'll let you. I'd take help from the devil himself right now."

He nodded. "Well, it seems you've set realistic expectations."

"I don't care who you are or what you're planning, if you can help Kevin."

Luella came back in time to save Cally from saying something truly ugly. She carried a handful of towels, plus a needle and thread she'd soaked in rubbing alcohol.

Marcus scrubbed his hands. At Bay's direction he reached for the needle and thread. "Let's get the party started."

Chapter Eleven

Thirty minutes later Marcus stood from his crouched position and flexed his cramping fingers. The bandage on Kevin's head covered eight ugly, uneven stitches, but they'd stopped the bleeding. His hands had shaken despite the good instructions Bay gave.

Marcus was grateful for those early patrol days when he'd ridden with the paramedics. Now if Kevin Tucker would just wake up, he would feel a lot better about him.

"Concerns me he hasn't woken up yet," said Bay quietly, echoing his thoughts. "He may have a concussion."

"What do we do if that's the case?" asked Cally.

"Nothing we can do here," said Bay. "Just wait and see."

Great. Another danger to add to the growing list. Besides the head wound itself, infection was also a concern. They'd sterilized everything as best they could, but it might not be good enough.

Marcus calculated the number of hours before Kevin might get to a doctor. Even if everything went according to schedule, it would be at least 6:00 a.m. tomorrow before Gregor let them go. Things could be getting dicey by then.

He wondered who Kevin was. A boyfriend, maybe. Cally had seemed willing to throw herself between him and Gregor's gun.

He was surprised and irritated to think she might have a lover. To imagine that they could have been together in the bed he was standing over right now. A split second later he identi-fied the feeling as jealousy and almost laughed out loud.

It was ludicrous that in the midst of the chaos they were in, he was worried about whether or not Cally was sleeping with someone. He tried to ignore how telling that was of his own feelings for her, but wasn't successful. He frowned as she leaned down to smooth Kevin's pillow. Yeah, he was hooked all right.

He moved back from the bed as Cally and Luella picked up the bloodied towels and makeshift bandages. They hadn't spoken to him the entire time he worked on Kevin other than to hand him the items he requested. Marcus didn't hold out much hope that Cally would want to speak to him now, either.

"At this point, the most important thing to do is watch for infection. Do you have any antibiotics here?" he asked.

Cally nodded. "Some Keflex I didn't finish when I had bron-chitis in January." There was ice water in her voice, but Marcus ignored that.

"Do you know if he's allergic to penicillin?"

"He's not. I've seen him take it before."

Marcus felt another stab of jealousy. He ignored that, as well.

"Good, try and get one or two down him in the next hour. You may have to melt the medicine and spoon it in. Whatever it takes." Marcus stopped, his reiteration of Gregor's words mo-mentarily stunning him. "I've got to go now. I'll check on him before I leave."

He didn't wait for a reply. He simply walked down the hall toward the kitchen. Not surprisingly, he heard soft footsteps behind him and turned to face Cally.

Those cornflower-blue eyes glittered; her voice was scath-ing. "Why are you doing this? I don't understand you."

Quite frankly, I don't understand myself at the moment. He couldn't very well say that.

"Don't try to understand me, Cally. There's no reason you should."

But she wouldn't let it go. It didn't seem to be in her nature. "Who are you, really? Because I don't believe for a moment you're like Gregor. I think you're playing at it."

Marcus returned her cool gaze and her eyes widened, "Omigod. That's it, isn't it? You're not who you say you are."

Marcus swore under his breath as he took her arm and pulled her into the nursery. They always seemed to end up in here. He shut the door and turned the lock.

He kept his hand on the latch and his back to her while considering his options. The first thought that ran through his head was he'd like to pick up where they'd left off on the pier.

He glanced over his shoulder. *Umm…probably not gonna happen.*

What in the hell was he supposed to do? If he told her the truth, even if she kept it to herself her change in attitude toward him could inadvertently give him away to Gregor. It could get them both killed. Harris, too.

But if he didn't tell her, she might keep questioning him in places like the hallway or on the dock this morning—places where they might be overheard. Or she might try and make another phone call that would end up getting them all killed. Gregor was a lot further over the edge than Marcus had initially suspected.

Telling her the truth might save her. Marcus no longer had a choice. Not really. With a heavy sigh he turned to face her.

She was staring at him with a mix of fury, curiosity and disdain that should have had him reaching to unlock that latch.

"No, I'm not who I say I am. I'm a police detective from Jackson here on an undercover assignment. I've been working with a special task force on Gregor's group for almost six weeks now."

She stared at him until the words registered, then gazed off into space. When she finally spoke her voice was strong but quiet. "If you're a cop and you've known the entire time this was going to happen, why didn't you stop them? Why haven't you stopped them already? What the hell have you been waiting for?"

"It's gotten complicated."

"What do you mean *complicated?*" Her voice rose, but she calmed herself before continuing. "They've got my son. They almost killed Kevin. What else do you need before you can stop them?"

"We'd… I'd planned on calling the governor's office in today—this morning—to set it up. We'd originally planned to catch them in the act. But now they've got Harris.

"Cally, this kind of operation can get really complicated. When they take down Gregor and his men, all four of them could get killed. Normally, that wouldn't be our biggest concern. But, normally, we don't have a kidnapping mixed up in the equation."

"What are you saying, exactly?"

"I'm saying that if I call the task force in and it gets messy, we may lose the only people who know how to get Harris back." *Alive* was his unspoken word.

Cally paled as she listened to Marcus's explanation, but her voice was still steady. "So what do we do?"

"I'm going to find Harris before the robbery, then we can call in the task force." He realized that answer might have sounded a bit too pat.

"But how are you going to find him?"

"I'm working on it. I've got someone helping me."

"But if you don't find him before the robbery, what are you going to do?"

"I suppose I'll have to do the job Gregor hired me for."

"Can you? I mean, as a cop, will they let you do that?"

Marcus thought through his answer carefully. Technically, no. He couldn't really help Gregor rob the casino. But he had every intention of doing so, if it would save Harris.

"Well, it's not the ideal, but it may be what's necessary."

"You mean you'd do this without telling your task force, don't you?"

"Yes."

"Why would you do that? Why would you risk that?"

Marcus didn't answer. He just stared at her intently.

Cally shook her head from side to side, clamping down on that lower lip he'd been fantasizing about. "But you don't know me. You don't know anything about me. You—"

A shout from the kitchen had them both swinging toward the door. Marcus unlocked it and followed the stream of curse words down the hall. The profanity grew more virulent the closer he got to the kitchen. He stopped in the shadows of the hallway.

Peter Sams was on the floor by the refrigerator flat on his back. Rob Johnson and Frank Boggs stood over him.

Marcus hadn't seen Boggs since the day before. Apparently, he had just arrived from wherever he had gone to take Harris. Marcus hesitated outside the doorway, hoping to hear where Boggs had taken the boy.

"What are you doing down there, Sams?" Johnson was asking.

"My back, you idiot, my back went out." Sams writhed on the floor, spitting the words.

"What did you do?" asked Boggs.

"Damned if I know. I just bent over."

"Like last month?"

"Yes, damn it. Just like last month."

"Want me to get Gregor?" asked Johnson, starting toward the kitchen door.

"Hell, no! You can fix it. But do it quick. This hurts like a son of a bitch."

"Man, Sams, I hate doing this crap."

"It's all right, I'll be fine if you'll just do it now."

"Okay, on the count of three." Johnson bent down beside Sams.

Marcus watched, fascinated in spite of himself. Johnson straightened Sams's legs and stood beside him at hip level.

After counting to three, he dropped onto one knee straight into Sams's abdomen.

There was an audible *crack* and a highly imaginative stream of expletives from Sams. Cally gasped.

Marcus didn't realize she'd been standing behind him all along. He turned and put a finger to his lips.

Johnson stood and reached out to help Sams to his feet.

"Works every time," said Sams, rubbing his lower back.

"Jesus, Sams, how do you stand it?" Marcus stepped into the kitchen.

Sams, Boggs and Johnson both looked over in surprise. None of them saw Cally creep back down the hall.

"Well, considering my options, I don't have much choice." Sams rolled his shoulders.

"What do the doctors say?" asked Marcus.

"Nothing I haven't heard before."

"They say it's okay to keep doing this?" asked Boggs.

"Hell, no. They've said one day someone will do a gut drop and I won't be able to stand up when they're done," he paused. "But what do they know? It works right now, and that's all that counts. I'll have it taken care of after this is over."

"You're one crazy SOB," said Johnson.

"They say that, too," replied Sams.

Johnson opened the refrigerator and tossed beers to Sams, Boggs and Marcus. On their way out of the kitchen they all had to step around the dark stain on the tile where Kevin had fallen.

Sams and Boggs followed Johnson into the foyer. "You coming, Marcus?" asked Boggs.

"No, I'm gonna get something to eat and go get cleaned up." He propped himself in the doorway.

"Don't tell Gregor about this, okay?" Sams popped the top on his drink. "I don't want him to worry about this happening tonight. He's edgy enough as it is."

"Yeah, sure. Whatever you say, Sams," said Johnson.

Boggs nodded his agreement as the three men drifted down the hallway toward the staircase, sipping their beers.

"See ya later, Marcus," said Boggs.

Marcus eased back to the kitchen, waiting until they were out of earshot before walking down the hall to find Cally. He found her in the nursery.

"So where do we go from here?" she asked.

He put the untouched beer on the dresser. "I've got to go to the casino and meet my contact. I want you to stay here, as far out of Gregor's way as possible."

"How will I know if you've found Harris?"

"I'll text you on your cell if Gregor and his men are still here. They can't monitor texts with their equipment. Or I'll send someone to tell you. Give me your number."

She shook her head. "Gregor took my cell last night. Luella and Bay's, too."

He pulled Kevin's phone out of his pocket and handed it to her. "What's his number?"

She rattled it off, and he entered it into his own phone.

"Okay, so you're set now. Don't let them see that phone and don't call the police with it. Remember the scanners. You understand?"

"I understand. When will you call the task force in?"

"After I know Harris is safe."

"I still don't understand why you're doing this…but thank you for…for putting my son's safety before your job."

Marcus couldn't meet her eyes and nodded instead. "I've got to go now. They'll be leaving here around midnight. Remember, stay out of Gregor's way. If you can't stay out of his way, at least do what he says without arguing. Don't antagonize him."

She muttered, "I'd like to shove his head in the oven."

Marcus smiled ruefully. "I know. But until things are under control, you cooperate with him. Agreed?"

She made a noncommittal sound.

"I've got to take a shower before I go. I'll see you before I leave." He paused a moment and looked straight at her. He had to get through to her on this.

"If things start to go bad, get out of here." He saw the protest in her face but kept talking. "Go into that cotton field across the road if you have to, but don't stay here. You've seen what Gregor is capable of. He's dangerous, especially with women."

"What do you mean?"

"He likes to hurt them." He let the impact of that settle. "If you have to, leave Kevin and go. Do you understand?"

She nodded slowly but dropped her eyes. He knew she wouldn't do what he said, but he'd had to ask her anyway.

"You never answered my earlier question," she said. "Why are you doing this?"

He stared at her without speaking.

I don't know. Because I care for you and your son. You make me feel things I didn't think I was capable of feeling.

Marcus didn't trust himself to answer that question out loud. He shook his head and had a vague sense of déjà vu as he left her standing alone in the nursery.

CALLY AND LUELLA took turns sitting with Kevin. In the late afternoon his fever shot up to 104 degrees, but they got it back down with rubbing alcohol and cool sponge baths. He still hadn't woken up, and that worried her. Bay had said it could be several hours before Kevin regained consciousness. The only positive thing about any of this was that she now had something to keep her mind off Harris.

All day she'd vacillated between trying not to think of her son and wishing Marcus would appear with him. She knew better than to expect him simply to drive up with Harris, but she'd hoped to have some word by now. As afternoon turned to evening, hope faded with the light.

At nine o'clock they served dinner to the men, or rather, Bay served dinner. He'd vowed earlier that neither Luella nor Cally would wait on them. Cally was washing dishes when Peter Sams came and said Gregor wanted to see her.

Her pulse quickened as she walked past the baby grand piano into the darkened library. One desk lamp shone in the oak-paneled room, casting eerie shadows on the wall and hiding Gregor's eyes. Pinpricks of sweat broke out on her upper lip.

"Mrs. Burnett, we'll be leaving River Trace shortly. I want to thank you for your hospitality."

He laughed that ugly, rasping sound she had grown to hate in the past twenty-four hours.

"I'm glad you've enjoyed yourself."

As soon as she spoke, Cally remembered Marcus's caution not to antagonize the man. But Gregor went on as though he hadn't noticed her sarcasm.

"It's certainly been entertaining. Although not as stimulating as I might have hoped," he said.

Narrowing her eyes, Cally lifted her chin. She knew what he was implying from Marcus's warning.

"Oh, Mrs. Burnett, don't be concerned. While I might have the inclination, I simply don't have the time."

She didn't relax her pose but felt some of the tension ease in her back. Gregor smiled. She still couldn't see his eyes, but she could hear the cruelty in his voice.

"All the same, I'd like to make the time later," he added.

Her chest tightened; she squared her shoulders. He was toying with her—just playing cat and mouse. Even that knowledge didn't stop fear from shimmying down her spine.

I refuse to let him know he's scaring me.

With startling clarity, she realized he relished using the polished, cosmopolitan gentleman's veneer as a weapon of intimidation. She glared defiantly at his shadowed face, knowing her stance was a sham.

She would do whatever Gregor asked to save Harris. She'd

proven what she was capable of last night in the nursery with Marcus. Still, something deep in her gut twisted at the thought of comparing what had happened there to what was happening here. Now.

"Hmm, no curiosity. That's not like you. Although, I don't suppose I actually know you all that well. On the other hand, Marcus certainly seems to know you—or would like to."

She blinked but didn't answer. She fervently hoped Gregor would tire of his game, tell her whatever it was he had to say and leave.

"I must admit he has excellent taste. But I don't think his technique is quite sophisticated enough for you."

There was another pause. He seemed to truly enjoy her unease. "Hmm. Well, no more time for chit-chat. I have some details to see to before we go."

"Mr. Williams, I've kept my end of the bargain. I haven't contacted the police or told anyone of your plans. When do I get my son back?"

"All in good time, Mrs. Burnett. All in good time. We actually need a little more help. You see, you're coming with us tonight."

She couldn't stop the involuntary gasp. "What? Why?"

He tilted his head as if talking to a small child. "I said that it might be necessary. You do remember that, don't you?"

She nodded numbly.

"Well, it's necessary."

"But…but why would you want to take me?"

"You're going to be a bit of an insurance policy for us with Marcus. Besides, you might be tempted to call the police or a doctor for your friend after we leave. This will remove that temptation. I don't think the Wigginses would risk you *and* Harris, do you?" He looked at her expectantly.

Cally shook her head woodenly. "No. They wouldn't risk both of us, I'm sure."

Her head was spinning. The thought *had* crossed her mind to at least call a doctor for Kevin after Gregor left. She might even have considered calling the police, despite Marcus's warning about things getting messy.

"But what can I do?" she asked. "Won't I be in the way?"

"Oh, I have something in mind. It's not too complicated. And I'd much rather have you with us than wonder what you might do after we leave. I'll explain it as we go along."

"After this will I get Harris?"

"Why, naturally, Mrs. Burnett, naturally."

Cally didn't trust his answer, but she knew it would be a waste of energy to protest anymore.

"When do we leave?" she asked.

"Aaah, now, that's the spirit. You be ready at twelve-thirty. You'll need to change into some clean clothes before we leave. You're going with us into the casino and don't want to draw attention to yourself. Frankly, you look like hell."

Cally glanced down at her stained jeans and blouse. She was wearing the same clothes she'd put on yesterday afternoon to clean the guest rooms. That seemed a lifetime ago.

She hadn't washed her face or brushed her hair since Sunday morning. Not that she gave a damn, but Gregor's description was depressingly accurate.

She hurried from the room, slowing only when she reached the hallway leading to her bedroom. *I am going to have to help them.*

She hadn't really thought it would happen, but she knew she could do it. She'd come to that conclusion this morning.

She walked into the bathroom and turned on the shower. Mechanically she stripped out of her clothes and climbed in. She shampooed her hair, turning her mind off as the water beat down. After showering, she dressed quickly and pulled her wet hair into one long braid. Slipping on her sandals, she felt surprisingly calm—considering what she was preparing to do.

It was surreal, like a newspaper article she'd read about another woman. "Preschool Mother Robs Casino to Save Son." Never in her wildest dreams did she imagine herself in this position.

Only this was no dream. Instead, it was a terrifying reality from which she couldn't escape.

Chapter Twelve

The hot air smelled like rain and felt sticky against her arms as Cally climbed out of the Suburban. Clouds scuttled across the normally brilliant night sky, allowing the full moon to peek through at short intervals. She was struck by how loud the night noises were: crickets, the occasional owl and the ever-present buzz of mosquitoes. Looking at the aging boat ramp reflected in the vehicle's headlights, she realized they were on one of the many finger lakes near the Mississippi.

The men pulled the tarp off the boat they had towed in and transferred three gun cases and a duffel bag from the truck. She recognized some of the gear from Gregor's room.

Working with military precision, no one spoke as they carried out their various tasks. Details had obviously been planned and refined over a period of time. Gregor stood beside her as the trailer was backed into the water off the ramp.

The boat was about twenty feet long and five feet wide. At first glance it appeared to be a large fishing boat, but the sides were higher and the bottom was flatter with a cabin structure in the center.

Cally's stomach churned from being so close to the river.

"It's a cab boat," said Gregor. "A bass boat with a few modifications. It has twin 225 Mercury motors and a reinforced hull." He sounded like a boy showing off his new bicycle.

"Is it safe?" she asked, trying not to let her fear of the water show.

"Of course."

Sams and Boggs eased the boat off the trailer. From behind her Johnson appeared, clad in a dive suit. He also wore a headset with a microphone wrapped around his jawline. A canvas scabbard ran down his back and a large handle stuck out of the top, resting between his shoulder blades.

Gregor stopped him before he headed toward the water. "Has the show started at Mattress World?"

Johnson checked his watch and nodded.

"What's going on?" asked Cally.

Gregor answered, the pride obvious in his voice. "Just our way of keeping local law enforcement out of our hair tonight. Mattress World is having a fire sale, so to speak. Within the next hour every person and vehicle in McCay County Emergency Services Department will be on-site at that company, which also happens to be located forty miles across the county from the Paddlewheel."

Cally felt her mouth shape a large "Oh."

"Johnson, we'll radio you when we get into position. Be at the loading dock no later than 0230."

She looked down at the illuminated face on her watch. It was 1:30 a.m.

"I'll be there," Johnson gave Gregor a quick salute before wading through the water and climbing into the boat. He disappeared into the cab and a moment later the engine started.

Sams unhooked the trailer and gave it a shove down the gravel ramp as the boat motored out of sight. The trailer sank just below the surface of the water. Everyone loaded back into the Suburban.

Moments later they were speeding down the gravel road. Cally looked back over her shoulder. To the casual observer there was nothing to indicate that they had ever been on the landing.

JOHNSON LANDED the boat forty yards downstream from the Paddlewheel. Directly in front of him was the service road leading to the casino's generator building. He had devices to set here before he could begin work at the loading dock. He started counting in his head to pass the time.

Fifteen minutes later he was opening his gun case. After attaching the suppressor, he pulled the Colt M4 carbine to his shoulder and took out the mercury vapor lights running along the river side of the casino. A series of soft "thumps" accented the tinkling of glass as the back of the building was plunged into darkness.

Next, he took aim on the loading dock's security camera. There was another "thump" as the camera shattered. He glanced at his watch. 0215. Right on time.

He dialed Sams's cell.

"You inside the perimeter?" asked Johnson.

"We're just waiting on your call. Go for it." Sams's voice was crystal-clear.

"Words I like to hear. I'm doing it now."

"I'll stay on the line till it goes dead."

"Roger."

He pulled the remote detonator from his duffel and toggled the switch. A half-mile away the bridge providing the only access to the Paddlewheel imploded. His cell connection to Sams was gone. The explosion took out the phone landlines and the cellular tower conduit that ran underneath the bridge.

Johnson had set the C-4 directly on the pipes holding the entire fiber-optic network. The Paddlewheel was now completely isolated and unable to communicate with the outside.

Johnson clicked over to the shortwave on his headset. "How'd it go?"

"Bridge is gone," said Gregor. "Repeat, bridge is gone."

MARCUS SIGNED the documents and handed them to Suzette Foster for her signature.

"Okay, that's the last cart from this drop. Has Randy signed off?" she asked.

He nodded.

"Good. We're gonna take our break before we start the count again. I need a cigarette something awful." The large woman rubbed an equally large hand over her face.

"Good idea," said Marcus. "Y'all have been going at it hard since nine-thirty."

"You, too. I appreciate you filling in tonight. Didn't you have a big whale coming in?"

Marcus shook his head. "Last-minute cancellation. Guy had to fly to Germany on some business deal. He'll be back next weekend."

Suzette nodded and checked the paperwork again.

Everything had to be checked, double and triple-checked here in the "soft count"—where all the paper currency was tallied. Next door was the "hard count" for coins.

An employee locker room was across the hall. Money was piled on all the tables—some was banded, some was loose. Along one wall a long countertop held machines that counted bills. It was rather stunning, but he'd become fairly immune.

Right now he was more concerned about getting in touch with Cally. She must be going crazy by now. Since Gregor and company were on their way here, he could call without worrying that her side of the conversation would be overheard.

He was going to have her contact Hodges and tell him every-thing. It was too late to stop the robbery, but the police would need a head start on finding the child if things went south here. And if Marcus called, he knew what Hodges would tell him.

Stand down until the cavalry arrived—don't go through with the robbery and don't go with Gregor. Marcus didn't like his boss, but he wasn't going to put Hodges in the position of giving direct orders that he had no intention of obeying, either.

Going through with the robbery was the only way of finding Harris. Marcus had seen enough of Gregor to know that the aftermath of robbing the 'Wheel was going to be ugly. These men could turn on each other, or they could all just disappear.

But he was fairly sure they were not planning to give the boy back. Going with them was the only way to find out where Cally's son was.

He studied the mountain of cash on the table before him. Larger denominations were counted by hand. Along another wall, carts from the 2:00 a.m. drop had just been collected and were waiting to be opened and counted. The casino had been so busy earlier tonight that they were still playing catch-up.

Security cameras mounted in the four corners of the room and the ceiling recorded everything but your thoughts. These cameras weren't hidden behind bubbles. They were in plain sight—no illusions of privacy and, therefore, no temptation.

Seven women and five men were counting. A double shift due to the holiday weekend, and all twelve were dressed in short-sleeved blue coveralls and flip-flops. Those who worked in the count weren't allowed to wear anything else.

Each employee was searched before entering and exiting the room, but theft was rarely a problem. There'd been a couple of instances involving only small amounts—no more than three hundred dollars. In every case, the employees had been fired immediately.

Suzette rechecked the numbers a final time while Marcus contacted the main security desk.

"We need another officer in the hard count. They're taking a break," he spoke into the two-way radio clipped to his shoulder.

"We'll send someone right down," came a static-filled reply. "Hey, Marcus, after that can you check out the loading dock? The cameras are screwed up again."

"How many are out, Ed?"

"Just one as far as I can tell. It gradually got darker then went blank."

"Sure, I'll check it. Buzz me through now."

A metallic click sounded as he knocked on the locked door and a sandy-haired security officer opened it. Security was always posted outside the counting rooms.

"Phil, the count's taking a break. You take care of the search. A female officer's coming to help. I've got to check on something."

"Sure thing," Phil stepped inside and began the required pat-down on the men.

CALLY LOOKED back at the decimated bridge as they sped toward the Paddlewheel. The explosion had made very little noise and it had been impossibly fast. One minute she'd been looking out the window, wondering why they'd stopped, and the next she'd heard a deep rumble that sounded like distant thunder.

"Right on time," said Sams, hanging up his phone.

Gregor nodded. "Johnson loves his work."

They drove on, both men pulling gear from the duffel bags beside them. Gregor slipped on a headset that looked like something a secret-service agent would wear.

"Bridge is gone. Repeat, bridge is gone." He spoke softly into the mike.

There was a pause; Cally assumed Johnson answered.

"Is everything in place?" Gregor was still speaking into his collar.

Cally tried to tamp down her nervousness about what was happening, focusing on the scenery to keep her mind off Harris.

The lights of the casino grew steadily brighter as they drove up to the entrance.

Where are you, baby? And where was Marcus? Had something happened to him? Had he found anything?

The lights almost hurt her eyes. The Paddlewheel looked as if it had been plucked straight off the Vegas strip and set in the middle of a Mississippi cotton field.

Rising out of the shadows, the casino had the appearance of the old-fashioned riverboats that had once graced the Mississippi a hundred years before. A large paddlewheel was at the stern with all the trappings of *Showboat,* though this motif was strictly a facade. Without the aesthetics it would have looked like a huge floating shoebox.

Mississippi riverboat gambling laws required that the gaming areas of casinos be "over water on the river side of the levee." A building did not necessarily have to be right on the Mississippi, in some areas the levee was several miles from the actual casino. According to the amendments, the body of water a casino sat on could be up to a half mile from the river itself.

The Paddlewheel floated on eighteen inches of water in a man-made pond, thirty yards from the river. When the 'Wheel had been built just before Katrina, there'd been all kinds of publicity in the newspaper. Cally had been fascinated.

A small canal had been dug off the Mississippi to float in two barges. Afterward, the canal had been closed, creating a large pond on which the barges were tied together and left floating.

The barge compartments were filled with concrete to anchor the structure, then they were covered with girders; the Paddlewheel was built on top. Water was constantly being pumped in from the river so the pond never went dry. There were several trailers and outbuildings behind the casino in addition to a road between it and the Mississippi.

Boggs parked in a darkened corner of the lot.

From his bag, Sams pulled a large handgun with what appeared to be a silencer on the end. He and Boggs also put on the unobtrusive headsets. Gregor handed an Atlanta Braves baseball cap to Sams and donned a Mississippi State one himself.

"Roger that," he said into his headset, then, to the men in the car, "Everything's in place. Let's test and synchronize now."

The men adjusted their watches and headsets as Gregor counted down to the minute.

"Johnson, Boggs will meet you at the loading dock at 0230. Any questions? Over."

Gregor tapped Boggs on the shoulder. No one spoke as they backed out of the parking space and pulled around to the brightly lit entrance. Gregor looked over at her as he opened the door. His eyes were lit from within. She wasn't sure if his enthusiasm was fueled from adrenaline or insanity—both options frightened her.

His voice rumbled, "All right, gentlemen, let's rock 'n' roll."

MARCUS STEPPED out of the counting room to head for the loading dock. Along the way he passed multiple security cameras and the telephone room, containing all the telecommunications and security wiring for the casino.

Passing through double doors, he arrived at the dock where another camera was mounted above the exit. He pushed down on the crash bar and walked outside, careful not to let the door shut behind him. Out of the camera's line of sight, he applied duct tape to the lock.

Boggs drove up alone in the Suburban just as Marcus was finishing. "Everything go all right?" he asked.

"Just like we planned," said Marcus. "What about y'all?"

Boggs nodded. "Everything's fine…so far. Where's Johnson? He's late."

"You're early," said Marcus. "He'll be here."

Before stepping back in view of the camera, Marcus pulled a small can of spray paint from his jacket. Reaching from underneath so he couldn't be seen, he sprayed black paint over the lens.

He let the door close behind him and waited. He didn't hear the usual "snick" of the lock. He pulled the radio from his shoulder clip, "Ed, I'm on the loading dock and I can't see anything wrong with the outside camera."

"Well, hell, that's just great," replied a static-filled voice. "The one inside the loading dock isn't working now. The screen's gone completely black, plus we're having trouble with the outside phone lines. What do you think is wrong?"

"I've got no idea. I'll check around and be back up in a few minutes. Could be the security panel in the telephone room."

Marcus stepped back onto the dock to unlock the large rolling door. He raised it as Johnson came jogging up with a duffel bag over his shoulder.

"Where are the dollies?" Boggs was pulling empty bags from the back of the vehicle and ignoring Johnson for the moment.

Marcus pointed to the far corner of the dock. "We'll need both."

"Hot damn. That's what I like to hear." Johnson climbed up beside Marcus.

"What about the laundry hamper?" asked Boggs.

"It's in the employee locker room across from the soft count," said Marcus. "We'll get it in a minute after I take care of the other cameras. Everything go okay?" he asked Johnson.

"Perfect. Everything's in place." Johnson had on street clothes now and slipped on a jacket from his duffel bag.

Marcus screwed a silencer on the end of his automatic. "I'll go take care of the hall cameras and the internal phones. After that you can come inside."

Johnson nodded.

Mindful of the cameras always watching, Marcus cruised back to the telephone room leaving both men on the dock to straighten out the gear. The keys to the lock on this door were kept in a secured cabinet in the cashier's office, so he placed the muzzle of his Beretta against the deadbolt and blocked the camera's view with his body. The lock disintegrated as the bullet ripped through the metal.

He was pulling out his cell phone and dialing Kevin's number at River Trace when it occurred to him—the bridge was gone. That meant all cellular and landline coverage was gone, too.

Everything had been taken out with the conduit explosion under the bridge. He looked down. *No Service* glowed brightly on the LCD screen.

He couldn't call Cally from here.

He muttered something foul and headed for the computer that ran the surveillance cameras. From the small laptop he could disable the entire system. He was in and out of the program within five minutes.

It took a bit longer to handle the internal phone lines. Lights were already blinking to indicate an outside line failure. Most of his time was spent unscrewing panels. Once inside the cabinets, he simply snipped a few wires and was done.

He had to make it look like the system was gradually failing to have Paddlewheel security buy the story. By the time they realized they were being robbed, it would be too late.

Walking back to the loading dock, he called surveillance on his radio. "Hey guys, how's it hanging up there?"

Ed Tate answered. "Holy smoke, Marcus. Thank God you called. The whole damn system is shutting down. What's going on?"

"Not sure. Could be some sort of plumbing thing. I just found water five inches deep in the west corridor. It must have shorted out something."

"You don't think we've sprung a leak, do you? Crap, that's all we need."

Marcus smiled grimly. He could imagine the thin man's

frazzled appearance at the other end of the radio. Ed drank Mylanta by the bottle, he was probably reaching for a new one right now.

"Hell, man, you're not gonna drown even if there's a hole the size of Texas in the hull. We're only floating on a foot and a half of water. Besides, I don't think it's a leak. More likely a water pipe busted. I'm gonna check out one more thing. Don't panic if you see some alarms going on and off, okay?"

"All right, Marcus, just keep us informed. Aw, man, the phones aren't even working now."

"Keep your shirt on. I'll get back to you."

Marcus clipped the radio back on his shoulder and headed back toward the loading dock. It was 2:36 a.m.

ASA DASHED out of Marcus's office and down the short hallway to the gaming floor. According to the plan, Marcus would have already let Boggs and Johnson in at the loading dock. There was no going back now.

It bothered him that Marcus wouldn't call Hodges. But Asa understood. If the task force was called in and things went south, a lot of innocent folks could get hurt—including the boy. But Marcus couldn't do it by himself. That's why Asa was there—to back up his partner.

Walking past the craps tables, Asa spied Manny Bledsoe. He had met Earleen's father several times when he'd been working undercover with Marcus at the Tonk. He and Manny had even shot some pool one night, drinking beer and commiserating over the trials of parenting. Manny's ideas about parenting were vastly different from Asa's, but he was as valuable a source of information as his daughter.

"How the hell are you, Manny?"

The big man looked up in surprise. "Oh, howdy, Asa. I'm okay, I suppose."

"What are you doing here so late at night? The Tonk burn down?"

Manny snorted a laugh. "Naw, I just closed up. Normally, I'd be home in bed right now. But Earleen...that crazy girl." He shook his head in exasperation.

Asa's eyes riveted to Manny's at the mention of Earleen. The bartender continued. "Well, you know she's been sick these past few days. Had a damn bad case of the flu. Thought she was gonna give it to me." Manny shook his head. "Then, today she takes on a babysitting job for Carlotta and Frank."

It was the last thing Asa had expected to hear, and he struggled to keep his facial features controlled as the story unfolded. His heart pounded while Manny ranted.

"Don't that beat all. Girl won't come to work in her daddy's bar this weekend when I really needed the help, but she'll keep some stranger's child for free. She doesn't even like Carlotta and that loser boyfriend of hers. Hell, kids. I don't know why she's doing it. But you know how it is. We've talked about this before."

Asa nodded, on automatic pilot.

"She tells me they'll owe her now. Why would she even want 'em to is my question." Manny shrugged.

"Where is she babysitting?" asked Asa, hoping he sounded calmer than he felt.

"She was supposed to keep the kid over at Carlotta's, but she got tired of that right quick and brought him home to our house for a while. Turns out the kid is sick. He's been crying all evening for his mama, and I think he's got a fever.

"Hell, I ain't going home to that mess. Had enough of that business with Earleen being sick last week. Anyway, she says Frank and Carlotta'll be there first thing in the morning to get him. So I figure I'll just gamble till daybreak, then go on home."

Manny's voice faded into the background of jangling coins and whistling bells on the slot machines.

Son of a bitch. The kid had been at Earleen's all afternoon.

"So what do you think?" Manny was staring at him. Asa realized he was waiting for a reply. To what question, he had no idea.

"I'm sorry, what'd you say?"

"Are the craps tables hot tonight?"

Asa had no clue, but he paused as if considering the question. He sure as hell felt lucky for the first time in forever.

"Yes, I believe they are. Go get 'em!" Asa raced away, not waiting for a reply.

He had to locate Marcus. Now.

He checked his watch and automatically reached for his cell as he sped across the gaming floor. By his calculations, Gregor and his men should be in the counting room sometime in the next ten minutes.

He wanted to find Marcus and tell him what was going on, but he didn't want to risk running into the middle of the robbery. He also needed to call Earleen and double-check about the child.

Was it really Harris Burnett?

Asa would have bet his life on it. Once he was sure, he could blow this thing wide open.

Chapter Thirteen

Cally stood at the gangplank entrance leading over the water into the Paddlewheel. Sams and Gregor were on either side of her. Turning to Gregor, she asked one last time, "Please, don't make me do this."

He shook his head. "You're helping us rob the casino, Mrs. Burnett. I thought you understood that." Gregor scowled, his look a mixture of impatience and condescension. "We've been over this already. It won't be difficult."

"Of course not," she muttered under her breath. He was insane. She felt the panic rising in her throat. The door opened, and Sams took her arm. The time for thinking was past as they sailed into the loud noise and bright lights of the casino.

The crowd was not as thin as one would have expected for two-thirty in the morning. Sams steered her across the gaming floor toward a bank of slots near the cashier's cage.

Gregor pulled out a stool and handed her a roll of quarters. The two men stood on either side of her, watching a set of swinging doors next to the cashier. Several men and women in blue coveralls were coming through the doorway, followed by a female security guard. Cally watched them cross the gaming floor and disappear into the crowd.

"We've got a couple of minutes before things get started.

Why don't you play some slots?" said Gregor. Cally recognized the suggestion for the order it was.

With shaking hands, she opened the quarters and began feeding them into the machine. All around her people were gambling, oblivious to everything except their own games of chance. She looked at the spinning fruits and numbers in front of her. This was like some kind of nightmare.

Everything moved in slow motion. Everything except her heart rate. Sweat puddled under her arms but her mouth was dry as cotton. Her hands felt too heavy to lift. Her fingers were clammy and she fumbled the change.

When she put in her fifth quarter, the bars rolled to sevens simultaneously. The bells on the one-armed bandit sounded and whistles began blaring. That seemed to snap the surrounding patrons out of their zombie state. People turned to watch as coins poured from her machine like a silver waterfall.

She couldn't seem to pull any air into her lungs and sat unmoving in shocked silence while perspiration ran between her shoulder blades.

Gregor put his arm around her and leaned over to whisper in her ear. "Smile, Mrs. Burnett. You've just won the jackpot."

He squeezed her shoulder in a vice-like grip and kissed her on the cheek—looking for all the world as if he was congratulating her. In reality, pain shot down to her wrist. She forced her lips to curve upward into a sickly grin.

Sams handed her several plastic token cups from the top of her machine so she could gather her winnings. Other gamblers turned back to their own machines as she scooped her coins out of the tray. A waitress came over to take their drink order.

"Let's cash Mrs. Burnett out," said Sams.

At the cashier's cage Cally watched the coins being tallied in a large hopper. She'd won seven hundred and fifty dollars. A casino employee carefully counted out the bills and slid them under the brass bars into her hand.

She stepped back from the cage and Gregor took her arm to lead her away, this time squeezing at the elbow. "It's time," he said.

He led her across the gaming floor and through swinging doors that read Employees Only. When the doors closed behind them, the noise was immediately muffled. They stood in a long hall with a security guard seated about three-quarters of the way down the corridor.

He was reading and didn't notice them at first. As they approached, he stood. The key chain attached to his belt jangled loudly.

"Can I help you?" His nametag identified him as Phil.

"Yeah," said Sams. "I think we're lost. We were looking for the restrooms."

"No problem," said the guard. He walked toward them, pointing in the direction they'd come from. "Just go back through those swinging doors and—"

As Phil directed them down the hall, Johnson came up from behind and hit him with the butt of his gun. Cally bit her lip to keep from crying out.

The guard crumpled immediately. Boggs caught him. Together he and Johnson dragged him across the hall into what appeared to be a locker room. Sams followed and propped open the door as Boggs and Johnson tied him up.

At the same time, Marcus jogged through double doors at the opposite end of the hall. He stopped short when he saw Cally. His eyes went wide then icy, hiding whatever he was thinking before he continued toward them pushing two dollies.

"What the hell is she doing here?"

"Last-minute adjustment," Gregor growled. "Deal with it."

She watched Marcus struggle for control and searched his face for any indication of whether or not he'd found Harris.

"Damn it, Gregor, we talked about your last-minute adjustments last night. You're going to screw this thing up yet."

Marcus parked the dollies beside a door labeled Soft Count.

He stalked past them into the locker room and returned seconds later with a huge laundry hamper on wheels.

Sams pulled a silenced automatic from beneath his jacket and pointed it at the soft count room's deadbolt. Cally jumped at the harsh metallic sound of the bullet tearing through the lock.

She looked up to see Marcus staring at her. Her heart threatened to leap out of her chest, but there was a warning in his gaze. He shook his head ever so slightly—no news. She struggled not to react.

The door opened with another gut-wrenching shriek and a shove when the torn lock raked across the metal facing. They got the dollies and hamper inside, and everyone but Marcus stopped in momentary shock.

"Damn," whistled Johnson. "That's a hell of a lot of cash."

Canvas bags filled with money and fitted with small padlocks were stacked at the far end of the room. Underneath the bags were several rectangular blocks of currency—counted, banded and shrink-wrapped. Several bulging garbage bags were heaped on the floor with bills peeking out of the tops. One table was piled high with uncounted bills.

The room was cool, as if the air conditioning had been left on too long. Marcus was so close behind her, Cally could feel heat radiating from his skin. Still she wished he was closer. As he pulled the door shut, more shrieking metal broke the spell.

She turned to him for a moment and he gave her a grim smile. "Let's get the party started."

The men immediately began gathering various sacks of cash. Boggs tossed the other men empty duffel bags for the loose bills, and Marcus shoved locked canvas sacks into the laundry hamper.

"This is more than I expected," said Gregor.

"Me, too," said Sams. "Maybe we won't have to hit the cashier's cage now.

"Of course we'll hit it," said Gregor. "Why wouldn't we? We have our diversion in place. Besides the cage has at least two million, maybe more. We aren't leaving it." He held out an empty sack. "Mrs. Burnett, we need your help."

"What?"

"You want your son back, don't you?"

"Of course." She took the bag without looking at him and picked up a stack of bills. The sheer volume of cash in the room made it seem like Monopoly money.

Marcus worked across from her. He didn't speak. He didn't have to. She knew he hated this for her. It was obvious in the way he was clenching his jaw.

She wanted to tell him it was okay. That she'd do anything to get Harris back. But of course, he knew that already.

She stared at him across the pile of money and made sure he saw the determination there in her eyes. Saw what she was prepared to do to any and all of these men. He had seen it last night.

When you needed to protect the people you loved, your pride, your standards became luxuries you really couldn't afford. Cally's pride and her standards had been the first casualties when her son's life was at stake.

She was surprised to see that the room was clearing out. Boggs shoved garbage sacks into the laundry hamper. Marcus and Johnson lifted the shrink-wrapped blocks onto the dollies.

"We gonna be able to make this in one trip?" asked Johnson.

"We've got to make it work," said Marcus. "I don't want to walk down that hall more than once."

"What about those?" asked Johnson, pointing to the four carts lined up against the side wall. They were twice as wide as a grocery cart and five feet tall. No way to tell how much money they contained and no quick way to get inside.

"Try your gun on the lock," said Gregor. "If that doesn't work, we'll have to leave them." Genuine regret filled his eyes.

"I hate the thought of that," said Johnson.

Gregor nodded. "Johnson, you and Marcus come with me to the cashier's cage. Marcus, get the guns Boggs brought in.

Sams—you, Boggs and Mrs. Burnett finish up in here. We'll meet you at the Suburban."

The men left as Sams nodded his agreement and went to work on the carts. Cally continued to fill her duffel with bills to put in the laundry hamper.

Fifteen minutes later they had all the carts emptied and the money loaded onto the dollies and hamper. Together they moved the money through the shrieking door and into the hallway.

Sams motioned Cally to go in front. "The first dolly will be easier for you to maneuver," he said. "It's not as heavy as the other. Let's move."

She pushed forward on cold steel handles. She was past the double doors and ten feet from the loading dock when Sams cried out behind her. She turned in time to see him fall, writhing on his back beside a cash-filled hamper.

MARCUS LED the way to the cashier's cage. He didn't like leaving Cally behind. Hell, he didn't like her being here, period. He was still trying to figure out how to get her separated from Gregor and away from this safely without blowing his cover or getting either of them shot when Johnson and Gregor followed him through the swinging doors toward the cashier's office.

He pulled the radio from his shoulder and called surveillance. "Hey, Ed. Can you buzz me into the cashier? I've got to get some keys. I think I found the problem."

"Hell, yes, I'll buzz you in. You figured it out?"

"Yeah, I'll know for sure in a few minutes, after I check on one more thing. The floor manager is meeting me here to open the key cabinets." He didn't blink as the lie slid off his tongue.

"Good. This crap's giving me an ulcer."

The door buzzed and Marcus, Johnson and Gregor stepped into a small holding room. The door closed behind them. The walls were Plexiglas. Marcie Adams, the head cashier, waved as she buzzed Marcus through the next door into the office.

"Hey, Marcus, you giving a tour or wha—" She stopped talking when she saw the guns in Gregor's and Johnson's hands.

The other cashiers turned to see what had stopped their usually verbose manager in midsentence.

"Don't try to stop us, Marcie. Just give us the money, and we'll be out of here with no one getting hurt." Marcus ignored the kick to his gut at the look of betrayal in her eyes.

"Marcus…I…don't understand how you could—"

"Shut up, Marcie, and back up to the wall," interrupted Gregor.

"Just do what we say, y'all. That way no one gets hurt," repeated Marcus.

He waved his gun toward the wall. The other employees joined Marcie as Gregor opened cash drawers and began filling an empty bag. Marcus watched the cashiers while Johnson went to work on the small safe in the middle of the room. The two customers in line at the far end of the cage couldn't see what was happening.

Johnson set a flexlinear C-4 charge and covered the explosives with a bulletproof vest before backing away. Gregor finished with the drawers at the far end of the office just as the clientele realized what was going on.

"Get down," said Johnson. He motioned to Gregor, Marcus and the cashiers. "Close your eyes and mouth. Cover your ears."

The small explosion sounded like a long string of firecrackers going off. Johnson immediately sprayed the inside of the safe with a fire extinguisher.

"We're being robbed!" Marcie screamed. Gregor popped her in the face with the butt of his gun and pointed his weapon at the other cashiers. Marcus grabbed his arm. "We don't have time for this, Gregor."

Johnson cleared out the safe as Gregor pointed his machine gun at the ceiling and squeezed off several rounds before pointing at the cashiers again. There was a wild look in his eyes.

"Come on, Gregor. Let it go," urged Marcus. "Johnson's

done." Gregor nodded once and headed for the door. Marcus and Johnson followed—racing out of the office, through the Plexiglas room and pushing open the swinging doors while pandemonium broke loose in the casino.

MARCUS, Johnson and Gregor burst through the double doors as Boggs was coming down on one knee into Sams's abdomen. Marcus heard the audible *crack* of vertebrae popping but no accompanying expletive. Sams's face went ashen. Cally stood to the side with an equally ashen face.

"Oh, shit," mumbled Johnson.

"Damn it, Sams. What the hell is going on?" Gregor exploded, pushing Boggs aside and kneeling by Sams's head.

"I don't…know what's…wrong. It popped…back into place earlier. But this time…I…still…can't…" He tried to lift himself and fell back on the concrete floor. "I'm having a hard time catching my breath."

"This happened earlier today and no one told me?"

No one answered.

"Damn you. I ought to leave your ass here." His hand gripped the handle on the machine gun and Marcus stepped in front of Cally. "Well, hell. If you can't get up, we'll have to carry you," spat Gregor. "The hamper is too full to put you in, too." He and Johnson handed their duffel bags to Marcus and raised Sams by his shoulders and feet. The injured man cried out when they lifted him.

"Ah Jesus, it's…never hurt…like this…before."

"I don't want to hear it," fumed Gregor.

If possible Sams's face grew whiter as they carried him toward the loading dock. Boggs pushed the cash-filled laundry hamper while Cally and Marcus brought up the rear with the dollies.

"What's going to happen now?" she whispered.

"I've no idea," said Marcus. "Just stay close to me."

She nodded. "You got it."

They laid Sams in the middle seat of the Suburban. His eyes were closed and Marcus wondered if he'd passed out.

"It's the best we can do for him right now," declared Gregor. "Get the damn money loaded."

The men went to work unloading the dollies and the hamper.

"It's going to be a tight fit." Boggs shoved a shrink-wrapped cube of cash into the back of the truck.

"There may not be room for all of us," agreed Johnson, pulling duffel bags out of the hamper.

"We'll damn well fit on two bench seats," snapped Gregor.

Marcus loaded the last of the cubes.

"All done here," Johnson and Boggs heaved the last two duffel bags into the back of the vehicle.

"Get to the boat," ordered Gregor. He was struggling to regain control. "Mrs. Burnett, you sit up front with Boggs and myself. Marcus, you and Johnson ride in back."

Marcus bit his lip against protesting the seating arrangements as they all scrambled into the SUV. There was no reason to fight that battle as Boggs roared away from the loading dock making the short drive to the river. Sams moaned when Boggs took a sharp left, backing the truck as close as possible to the boat.

Before the Suburban had stopped, Gregor was out. Johnson and Boggs followed. Marcus took Cally's hand to help her off the running board. "Stay next to me," he whispered again. She nodded. The fear in her eyes was reflected from the headlights. Still she helped the men unload and stack all the canvas and duffel bags along the starboard side of the boat.

Garbage sacks and shrink-wrapped cubes went in the bow. Smaller canvas bags were piled on top of the duffels on the right-hand side. Johnson and Boggs moved Sams to the craft and laid him flat on the deck. He seemed to come around a bit but still couldn't move his legs.

Headlights flashed over them. Cally looked up as she handed the last bag of cash to Boggs. A car was speeding along the service road toward the dock. Gregor lifted her up and over the side, shoving her into the boat. She landed with a thud on her hands and knees, scraping a good two layers of skin from her knuckles.

There wasn't much room for her to maneuver with all the money and Sams laid out down the middle. She was shoved against the duffel bags and Sams's legs. She'd avoided boats and the water since Jamie's accident. The fear factor of all this was nauseating her. She held on to the seat in front of her and concentrated on not throwing up.

Everyone climbed aboard while Johnson gave the boat one final shove. Boggs and Johnson stayed up front. Marcus made his way to Cally behind the cabin and put his arm around her as Gregor started the ignition and backed away from shore with a lurch. A small canvas sack tumbled over the side.

"Watch it!" Gregor warned through the open cabin window. "Grab that bag!"

Johnson leaned over and tried to snatch it out of the water, but he was too late. The pouch plummeted beneath the surface as soon as it hit.

"Watch what the hell you're doing!" shouted Gregor.

"Yes, sir. If you'll watch where the hell you're going." Johnson looked at his watch pointedly and scrambled to the stern. Once there, he dug under some gear and pulled out a small black box.

Cally was deep breathing through her mouth, desperately trying not to hyperventilate. She was grasping her side of the boat so tightly her hands ached.

She saw Gregor at the wheel through the rear of the cab. He had them out in the rapidly moving current almost immediately. She looked toward the Paddlewheel.

The car that had followed them was parked at the river's edge. Next to it was their abandoned Suburban. A man stood in the headlights' reflection.

"Who's that?" asked Boggs.

Everyone except Johnson looked toward the shore.

"Probably securi—"

One explosion after another ripped through the night drowning out Marcus's reply. A blast from the generator plant lit up the sky as a fireball shot seventy-five feet into the air. Even on the river they felt the shock waves.

Instantaneously, the lights of the casino disappeared.

The car they had been watching flipped backward as the Suburban blew apart and exploded into flames. The man who had been reflected in the headlights was no longer visible.

Debris shot into the air and rained down into the water. Cally screamed as several smaller explosions detonated in the generator plant. The hellish flames and smoke reflected in the water surrounding them.

There seemed to be no escape.

Chapter Fourteen

Horrified, Cally stared at the shoreline as the sounds of reverberating explosions faded. Her head rested against one of the
duffel bags as if on a pillow, even though she couldn't breathe.
Weight on her chest crushed the air from her lungs.

Marcus had thrown himself on top of her as flaming debris
rained down. His arms partially covered her face, but she could
still see the generator plant burning.

"You okay?" He sat back on his knees and reached for her
hand, holding it tightly between his fingers. The sky was so
bright, it looked as though dawn was breaking at 3:00 a.m.

"No, should I be?"

He shook his head and leaned back down to speak, his words
stirring the air by her face. He whispered despite the roar of the
boat's engine. "You shouldn't even be here."

"I didn't have a choice."

"I know.

"Do you have any idea where Harris is?" She kept her voice
low. Marcus helped her back onto the seat beside him.

"I couldn't find anything. That's why I didn't contact you."

"It's why you had to go through with this, isn't it?"

He didn't answer but kept hold of her fingers—rubbing the
tops of her hands so softly, it was almost erotic. The feelings
he stirred in her were so out of place, she didn't recognize

them at first. The lights of the fire faded as the boat moved swiftly downriver.

"Why are you doing this?" she asked.

He took a long time and a deep breath before answering. "I told you last night. Spending time with Harris, with you. It wasn't an act."

She peered at him through the darkness, wishing now for the brightness of the casino fire so she could see his eyes as something unfurled deep inside her.

A little mortar crumbled in the huge wall around her heart, the wall she'd built when Jamie died. The wall she'd kept intact since her child had been born.

She wanted to weep for their timing, for herself, for Marcus—but mostly for Harris. None of this mattered if she didn't get her son back.

The entire experience was surreal, like some high-octane action movie. Except it was happening *to* her. She had no real sense of time anymore, but felt the air become markedly cooler when Gregor steered them further toward the center of the river.

The running lights were dimmed and a faint glow illuminated the water in front of them. Occasionally a floating branch or some other type of debris bumped the side of the boat. Springtime on the Mississippi brought all kinds of interesting objects into the river.

Inside the boat, Sams moaned occasionally. His head was propped on one of the bags; he seemed to drift in and out of consciousness.

Marcus kept holding her hands. The warmth of his palms on her frigid fingers was more than comforting. He was making her melt a little more each moment.

Part of her was grateful for the distraction from their wretched reality, another was mortified. She shouldn't be attracted to this man. Not here, not now.

Squeezing her eyes shut, she tried to imagine herself somewhere else.

Harris. I'm in the nursery rocking Harris to sleep. She could almost smell the baby lotion and little-boy scent.

A hard jolt had her eyes flying open.

"Grab those bags!" Gregor shouted at Boggs and Johnson.

She watched in stunned disbelief as a massive tree trunk with branches and roots still intact slammed into the boat. The concussion on the port side rattled her teeth and knocked Marcus off the seat.

A grinding mechanical sound buzzed like a small chain saw as the boat heeled crazily on its side. Duffel bags and shrink-wrapped packages slid into the water while the boat continued to tip almost completely over.

"Grab the money!" Gregor cursed viciously.

Boggs and Johnson dove toward her, grabbing wildly for the canvas sacks. She stood, struggling to hang on to the side and move out of their way at the same time.

"Sit down, Cally!" shouted Marcus.

The boat rocked to port and came down with a splash.

"Marcus!" She was airborne, falling backward and clawing at nothing.

Milliseconds later icy water closed over her head, filling her mouth and nose. Paralyzed with fear, she didn't kick when the eddy pulled her down.

She was drowning.

THE SECOND JOLT threw Marcus onto his bad shoulder. His arm ached under the best of circumstances, but this was excruciating. His heart stopped when Cally tumbled over the side.

Gregor swerved starboard to avoid another collision, but that caused the tree's roots to jam between the twin motors and the back of the boat, knocking the craft sideways.

Now the boat was wedged on top of the tree and rolling from

port to starboard. At the same time it turned in lazy circles like a carousel ride gone mad. Johnson and Boggs scrambled to keep the money from falling overboard. Marcus watched as another canvas sack slipped through Boggs's hands; the man turned the air blue with curses.

"Hang on to those bags, damn you!" growled Johnson.

"I'm trying, you bastard. I'm trying," muttered Boggs.

Sams flipped over on his face, his cries muffled by the deck.

"One of you, come help me steer!" shouted Gregor.

Marcus ignored them all to scan the water. "Cally! Cally, where are you?"

He couldn't see anything as the boat careened from side to side. It rocked almost all the way over to port and slammed back to starboard. They could capsize any second.

Sams was tossed back and forth as the boat teetered on the tree trunk. On one particularly wild swing, he fell over the side into the water. "Help me!" he screamed.

Johnson reached out to grab him, but Sams couldn't kick and kept sinking beneath the surface.

"I'm caught in the branches. I can't move! I'm gonna drown! Help me!"

Boggs started to help but saw that the money would keep going over the side if he left it. "Marcus, you gotta help him. I can't leave the bags."

The tree wedged itself more firmly between the motors, sliding further under the boat. The branches were pulling Sams under. He couldn't kick himself free because his legs were paralyzed. Johnson hung on to him, but this was a losing battle.

Where was Gregor?

Marcus didn't hesitate. With his good arm he grabbed a life vest from under the seat and tossed it to Johnson. Grabbing two more, he climbed to the stern.

"Cally? Cally, answer me!"

How far back was she?

Damn it. He had no idea, and no choice but to go in after her. He prayed she wasn't tangled in the branches like Sams.

Ignoring the pain in his shoulder, he braced himself against the side of the boat and slipped on the vest. He had to time the jump exactly right to avoid the propellers and the tree. He waited till the boat swung back to starboard, took a deep breath, and dove in.

Chapter Fifteen

At first Cally couldn't tell which way to swim for the surface. Something struck her on the head and shoulder as she struggled to orient herself. A moment later she realized it was a canvas bag of money. So, up was that way.

Sputtering and gasping for breath, she pushed her head above the surface and treaded water. The boat was twenty yards in front of her, seesawing wildly on a tree trunk. Still gagging from all the river water she'd inhaled, she tried calling for help but could manage no more than a croak.

The taste of grit was bitter. Men's voices carried on the water, shouting to keep the boat upright and the money inside. Marcus called her name over their shouts and obscenities.

"Cally! Where are you? Cally?"

The boat slid further away and she felt the panic build inside. This was her nightmare—drowning on the river like Jamie. In her mind's eye she saw the water closing over her head, pulling her down...down. She could actually visualize herself going under the waves—feel the pressure in her chest as she fought for air.

"Marcus! Marcus, help me!" Her voice was a whisper.

The running lights disappeared and stygian darkness closed in around her like a heavy blanket. She was a good swimmer and knew logically that she could tread water for several hours if need be. But once the voices faded into the night, her fear of the river began to win over her common sense.

It wasn't just a matter of swimming to shore. It was the eddies, undertows, currents and snakes she would have to contend with on the half-mile swim.

You're not going to drown. Kick your shoes off and swim, damn it. She was getting her sandals loose when she heard loud splashing several yards in front of her.

"Cally? Where are you?" Marcus's voice was clear and strong. Relief washed over her and she stopped struggling with her shoes.

"Marcus. Marcus I'm here!"

MARCUS WAS on the ragged edge of frantic by the time he reached Cally. He wanted to pull her into his arms. He'd been so convinced she was gone.

He was grateful for the darkness as he slipped her into the lifejacket. He didn't want to give away the white-hot panic he'd felt moments earlier as he'd watched her tumble over the side. It would be obvious if she saw his face.

"You okay?" he worked to keep his voice even, hissing as he tightened the straps across the front of her vest with one hand.

His shoulder hurt like hell, but that didn't matter right now.

"You came after me." There was wonder in her voice.

"Are you okay?" he repeated, breathing hard.

He was breaking all his rules, but he couldn't help himself. His hand brushed her cheek. He stopped a moment to lift her chin and study her face.

Clouds scuttled across the moon so she could only catch a glimpse of his intense expression.

"I…I think so…you dove in after me. Why'd you do that? What happened?" She babbled, obviously astounded at what he'd risked to come after her.

He held on to her chin a beat longer. In another time, another place he'd kiss her. Here it was insanity.

But he kept staring at her mouth. She had to know what he was thinking.

She stopped talking. Earlier, he'd meant what he said. He did care.

She reached up to put her hand over his. The life jackets kept their heads above water whether they kicked or not. Her mouth formed a silent *Oh*. Now she really knew.

"Believe me, Cally, diving overboard wasn't that heroic. A tree slipped under the stern and drove us sideways. They'll be lucky if they don't capsize."

"No!" Water splashed in her face but she kept on talking. "If they drown, what'll happen to Harris?"

"Don't think about that right now. We've got to concentrate on *us* not drowning," he paused, still catching his breath. "It's a helluva swim."

"Where are we?"

"That's a good question. I don't know. But the current is going to take us quite a distance as we go in. We'll figure it out when we get to shore."

"Are you a good swimmer?" she asked.

He nodded. "Pretty fair."

"Me, too."

"All right then. Let's get the party started."

She snorted a bleak laugh.

BATTERED BY the icy current and constantly bombarded with all kinds of debris, they headed toward the eastern shore. Swimming in spurts, they didn't speak, focusing instead on the task before them.

Cally was confident in her ability to get to shore but got spooked when something slimy shimmied down her arm. If she stopped to contemplate snakes right now, she'd flip out. So she ignored that frightening possibility and kept moving forward.

The life jackets made progress awkward, but the security they provided more than made up for the decrease in efficiency.

Her eyes adjusted to the darkness and she saw the shoreline in the distance. She didn't know how long they'd been swimming, but it seemed like hours. In reality it had probably been no more than thirty minutes.

She didn't bother asking how much further. The bank didn't appear any closer than when she'd first spied it. Whenever they stopped, he'd touch her, talk to her. Keep her calm.

"How you doing?" asked Marcus.

"Hanging in there," she gasped. "But I'd rather be catering a wedding."

"I didn't realize you did catering, too."

"Don't that often. I need to hire more help when I do."

"What kind of help?" he asked.

"Why? You looking for work?"

He laughed. "I've no idea what my job is going to look like when this is over."

She couldn't believe they were having this conversation. They might have been sitting on a park bench, instead of trying to keep from drowning on the river.

They rested three more times on their way in. At each stop, he talked as if it were the most natural thing in the world to be treading water in the middle of the Mississippi. After their second breather, Cally realized he was talking to keep her mind off the scary things out there with them.

Her arms ached and her eyes were burning when they finally neared the bank. Because of the flooding, the trees near the shoreline were under water with their jagged tops just clearing the surface. Swimming closer, they had to float with their legs behind them to avoid being caught in the branches below.

"Watch out for snakes," warned Marcus.

"Don't even say that out loud."

Now, snakes were all she could think of.

This kind of brushy bank was ideal for cottonmouth water moccasins—an aggressive, deadly snake with a distinctive swanlike profile on the water. She couldn't imagine anything worse than running into one here.

"Let's head for the break in those trees." He squeezed her hand, distracting her from that disturbing train of thought.

At the muddy bank he reached to help her up; she landed in a heap on top of him. Her wet clothing clung like a coating of ice, but she barely noticed the discomfort. Grateful to be out of the river with no snake encounters, she felt drunk with relief.

Gravel crunched under their bodies as she tried to move, but Marcus put a hand on her waist. "Do you have any idea where we are?" His breath was warm on her frosty cheek.

"Out of the river?" She turned to face him, giddy with the fact that they'd survived the swim.

"Cute."

Smiling into his eyes, she started to roll off; but again he stopped her, this time putting a hand on her face the way he had in the water. She was suddenly very aware that she was sprawled on top of a man.

"You're bleeding." He wiped her cheek with his fingers.

"I imagine we both are after all the junk in that water. We probably need tetanus shots, too."

Her breath hitched when his other hand slid more firmly around her waist. Warmth pooled low in her tummy—an almost foreign sensation.

The wind scraped the clouds away from the moon, and she could see his eyes clearly. Those chocolate-brown irises were no longer teasing but filled with heat, a very male response evident beneath her hips.

He was studying her, but he wasn't looking for another bump or scratch on her face. He leaned in closer and she didn't pull away.

"Tell me now if you don't want me to kiss you," he murmured.

She stared at him, unable to answer, looking for something in his eyes.

"Is this what you want?" His voice was soft.

Heat was stirring in her, driving her like it hadn't in what seemed like forever. She still couldn't answer, so she did the next best thing.

She put her hand on his at her waist and lowered it. His laugh sounded a bit strangled as she leaned down to kiss him, finally finding her own voice.

"You talk too much, Marcus."

He cupped her butt in his hands, slipped his tongue between her lips, and pulled her against the hard length of him. She tasted river water and mint on his breath.

"Okay, I'll shut up now. It's just…you shock me, a little." He smiled before he kissed a line along her jaw and down her neck.

Tiny shudders rippled throughout her body. "Hmm…well, you know what they say about those who are easily shocked, don't you?"

She reached down to unbutton his jeans, her fingertips on the zipper. "They should be shocked more often."

"That wasn't a complaint. Strictly an observation."

His low laugh had her fingers sliding off the zipper pull as he rolled her to her back where the ground was soft. She could smell the rich soil, but she didn't care where she was when he slipped his hand between her thighs and touched her through her wet capris.

All joking fell by the wayside as they pulled at each other's clothing. She tunneled her hands in his hair as he skimmed his hands along the sides of her breasts. He was kissing her, unbuttoning her blouse and she was lost in the sensations, forgetting everything except the feel of his hands and lips on her body.

He had her shirt off when the sound of the moving water registered. *The river. Jamie. Harris.*

Oh God. What was she doing? The cold rush of reality hit. Frantic, she pushed against his chest.

"No. I can't…be…here. Doing this." She tried to sit up and Marcus had to, as well.

His hands were instantly still. "Are you okay?"

"I'm sorry. It's Harris and the river. I just… I can't." Scrambling away from him, she crossed her arms over her chest.

He handed her the blouse he'd just taken off her and she slipped it on, embarrassed at what she'd almost done.

"Cally, it's all right. I understand. We need to keep moving. We've got to get to a phone."

She struggled not to laugh hysterically. He understood? How could he possibly, when she didn't understand herself?

She rubbed her arms; the chill of what she'd forgotten while she'd been kissing this man frightened her. "I'm sorry."

"For what? Almost having sex with me?" He nodded to the place they'd both been lying a moment before. "That's nothing to be sorry for."

"No, it's just. This was a mis—"

He held up his hand. "This was 'survivor instinct.' The God-I'm-so-glad-to-be-alive-I've-got-to-screw-someone-right-now sex. Okay? It was nothing more than that. Don't feel guilty about it."

Huh? That was not how she was seeing this. "I don't think I can dismiss it like that."

"You're going to have to until we get out of here. I'm sure you can do that." There was an edge to his voice now.

Appearing completely unselfconscious, he stood and zipped his jeans. She struggled not to stare. This had meant that little to him? It had meant something to her…that's what was scaring the bejesus out of her. It meant too much.

"Do you have any idea where we are?"

Marcus was acting as if they'd just had high tea here at the river's edge instead of whatever it was they'd very nearly done.

She was still trying to wrap her mind around it, but obviously he didn't want any more analysis. They had to keep moving. This was happening way too fast.

She focused on his question. "I think we're close to Stewart Landing. If we are, there's a road right behind us that leads over the levee. We'd be right outside the gate to the hunting camp my husband belonged to."

"Palmers?" Marcus wouldn't look at her.

"Yeah, how'd you know that?"

He shook his head. "It's where Gregor is meeting his get-away plane."

"On the airstrip?"

"That's the plan."

"Well, he *is* deranged. After all the flooding this spring, the soil on the strip won't be able to handle the weight of a plane."

"What do you mean?" He finally made eye contact, his coffee-colored eyes boring into her.

"That was one of the big complaints from out-of-town members. They couldn't fly in when the river got up to a certain point even if the strip wasn't covered."

"I don't understand."

"When the Mississippi comes over the embankment, the land next to the water becomes so saturated it practically percolates. You or I could walk across and it would seem perfectly stable, but try to drive a truck or something heavy across and it will sink to the axles."

In the semidarkness Cally could see Marcus's cold smile. "You're sure about this?" he asked.

"Yes. The strip is on a field next to the river. It may look safe and dry, but it's not."

"Gregor won't be able to use his plane, even if he gets to the airstrip?"

"Not after the floods we've had these past few months, no."

"So he'll be stuck out here at the hunting camp, or he'll be back on the water." Marcus wrung out his socks and slipped his shoes back on. "I've got to get to a phone. How far are we from town?"

"About ten miles from Murphy's Point."

"How about Palmers? Can we get there from here?"

"If the river wasn't up, we could just walk in. But with it so high, the only way in is by boat. Right now even the caretaker has to come in and out by the river."

"How do members get to their cabins when it's like this?"

"They use boats, too."

"Where do they put in?"

"Right here. It saves time if they leave them at the landing. That way they don't have to haul them back and forth from town. See, there's one." She pointed to an indistinct hump ten feet away.

"How long does it take to get into the camp from here?"

"Probably fifteen minutes, more or less. But wait a min—"

"That's great," interrupted Marcus.

"I don't like what you're thinking. It's extraordinarily dangerous to go out there in one of those things even if you know what you're doing."

He barked a laugh. "After what we just did, I think I can handle it."

"We were extremely lucky. I don't want to go back out there again."

"You won't, I will."

"Marcus, you can't do this by yourself—at night, not knowing the area. You could get hung up in brush or flip over."

"I'll be fine." He stood and headed to the boat.

"You don't even know where you're going."

She scrambled up to follow him, picking her way carefully since her feet were bare and her ankle was still sore. He turned the small vessel right side up and began shoving it toward the water.

"My husband drowned on this river in one of those boats. Please don't do this."

He was hooking the motor to the fuel line and stopped to look at her. "I'll be all right. Trust me." He bowed his head and went back to work.

"Damn you. That's exactly what Jamie told me the morning he drowned." She hesitated, appalled at her outburst. The stress from the almost-sex, her worry for Harris, for Marcus, for everything imploded. She couldn't seem to stop the words from spilling out.

"I begged him not to hunt on the river. The water was too high. It was dangerous, but he went anyway and he died. And that left me…that left me alone to pick up the pieces."

She was waving her arms, beyond caring if her words were coherent. "How in hell can I trust you? I don't even know you and you're doing something stupid like this, when I'm begging you not to. What will you do when you get there? Even if the plane has landed, how are you going to stop them? You couldn't possibly have a plan for this."

Marcus's voice was gentle, quiet. "I'll find out where Harris is."

"How can you—" She stopped in mid-sentence.

Why was she yelling? Her anger had nothing to do with Marcus. He was still trying to save her son.

She closed her eyes and shook her head. The person she was mad at was…Jamie. Jamie, who had left her with a farm heavily in debt and a baby on the way.

He hadn't meant to leave her in such horrible shape. The rational part of her knew that. But the day he'd died, all her carefully laid plans for permanence and security had crumbled in the dust. She'd been so frightened and so…furious. But she'd never really admitted the anger to herself or anyone else.

Instead, she'd stubbornly rebuilt that elusive stability for herself and Harris—until Gregor came and took it all away. That's where the anger was coming from. She was livid and consequently mortified by her tirade—everything felt totally out of her control.

Despite her embarrassment, she knew she'd just figured out something terribly important. Unfortunately, she didn't have time to examine all the implications right now. She chewed on her lower lip.

"God, Marcus, I'm sorry. I know you're trying to help." She stared toward the river and felt it moving beyond her range of vision. Just like she felt Marcus's eyes on her, only she couldn't bring herself to look up at him.

"I hate to lose it. I really do. You wouldn't know that from these past few days. I've completely fallen to pieces."

"Don't you realize how strong you are? What you've been dealing with the past twenty-four hours alone would crush most people."

She wasn't sure what she heard in his voice, but it wasn't pity. He reached out to touch her as she asked the question he had yet to answer. "Why are you doing this?"

He didn't say anything at first and she stood there a moment—uncertainty fading as the truth finally dawned on her. This man truly cared. And he was willing to risk his life to find Harris, just as he'd risked his life to save her on the river.

"This is real for me, Cally. I'm not playing a part." His hands were warm on her river-soaked shirt.

"But you don't even know me."

He laughed and she cringed at her poor choice of words.

"Well, not really…biblical definitions aside," she clarified.

"I know enough, and I knew enough before we *almost* had sex. You do whatever it takes to protect the people you love. But don't idealize me, Cally. If you really knew me—what I've done—you'd run like hell."

He stared at her through the darkness and the breeze picked up around them. Finally, light broke through clouds to shine on his face. The stark look of need in his eyes sent a tingling awareness down her arms.

He let go of her suddenly as if she burned his hands, but she could feel the heat of his gaze through her wet clothing. She couldn't turn away and stared back. This wasn't about "survivor sex" anymore. An owl calling in the night broke the spell.

"I don't run," she said, shaking her head to clear the scattered thoughts. "I'm going with you. No arguments."

He started to say something, but stopped.

She tried to ignore him as she bent down to help push the boat into the water. Her hands shook; her heart pounded. Marcus now made her extremely nervous for an entirely new reason.

"I'll take you as far as the caretaker's, but I go to the airstrip alone," he said.

She didn't answer and stepped into the small boat to take a seat at the bow. He climbed in behind her. After two false starts, the motor sputtered to life. Neither of them spoke as he steered through the gnarled treetops back onto the river.

"GREGOR. Where the hell are you?" shouted Johnson.

Gregor staggered to his feet in time to see Marcus dive off the end of the boat. He shook his head to clear his vision.

Big mistake. His skull felt as if he'd had been hit with a two-by-four and his arm hurt like hell. It had to be broken. He wasn't sure how long he'd been out, but he could hear Johnson calling his name and cussing Frank Boggs.

"Boggs, you sorry SOB, you gotta help me, man. I can't do this by myself."

Boggs clung to the canvas bags, shaking his head. Only a few sacks of money were left. All the shrink-wrapped cubes were gone.

"You bastard," shouted Johnson. "He's gonna drown if you don't help me."

Gregor tripped over a paddle and stumbled out of the cabin. Johnson was hanging on to Sams's arm, trying to pull him free of the branches.

"Gregor! Gregor, help me." Sams was steadily sinking

lower in the water when Johnson shoved a life preserver under his arms.

"I need to go in to cut him loose," said Johnson. "The life preserver isn't going to help much. The tree is pulling him under the boat."

Gregor raised a skeptical eyebrow but said nothing as he held on to Sams with his good arm. Johnson drew a long-handled machete from the scabbard down his back and slid into the river. Careful to avoid becoming tangled in the branches himself, he began hacking at tree limbs.

Gregor realized immediately that this wasn't going to work. Sams did, too, and grew more panicky as the boat seesawed on the tree, causing him to slip further under the waves. His face was now almost completely submerged.

"Jesus...I'm drowning...Johnson...Gregor...you gotta help...me..."

The boat continued to pitch and revolve. Johnson kept hacking at branches because there was nothing else to do but watch Sams drown. The faster he cut, the faster Sams went under.

Gregor tried to calm his friend, but Sams knew he was going to die. Unwilling to quit, Johnson threw the machete aside and tried pulling at Sams's shoulders. But it was no use. The man's legs were shackled by the branches and being relentlessly pulled under the boat. Johnson couldn't budge him.

Sams wept and shouted whenever his head was above water. His hand gripped Gregor's like a vise. The nightmare seemed to go on forever, but, in fact, it was over within three minutes. Sams went under for the last time with Gregor still holding his hand as his fingers went slack. Johnson kept trying to free him until the very end.

"He's gone," said Gregor.

Hurling vicious curses at Boggs, Johnson hauled himself back into the boat.

"I could have saved him if we'd started earlier. You just

stood there and watched him drown. I'm gonna kill you with my bare hands!"

"What was I supposed to do?" Boggs whined. "Let it all go overboard?"

Johnson answered with a blow dead center to the man's abdomen. The air whooshed out of Boggs's lungs as he doubled over.

Johnson reared back to hit him again, but Boggs came up with a right cross, knocking Johnson back and over one of the aluminum benches. Still holding on to Sams's arm, Gregor didn't interfere—even when one of the canvas bags began to slip over the side. Boggs turned to grab it.

Johnson stood and when Boggs swung back around, the black man hit him again with an upper cut just as the boat tipped. Boggs fell backwards across the bags. His head connecting with the side of boat sounded like a melon bursting. Boggs didn't move.

Gregor watched blood gush and pool on the duffel bag below from the gash behind Boggs's ear. He was still breathing, but Johnson didn't bother to check the man's pulse. He simply pulled him off the sacks and sank down onto one of the benches with his head in his hands.

"That son of a bitch. He got what he deserved," muttered Johnson.

Gregor didn't answer, but Johnson was right. Boggs didn't matter a damn. Gregor had known Peter Sams twenty years. They'd gone on hundreds of missions together. Sams had probably considered Gregor his closest friend. He had saved his life more than once.

His death was a senseless waste and right as he was about to have it all, too. But Sams had also been pigheaded and stubborn. This whole back thing had been a result of his obstinacy.

Friendship or no, Gregor would have wanted to drown the man personally if he'd screwed up the robbery. So actually this was Sams's own fault anyway. With a heavy sigh, he let go of the lifeless hand and turned to more important matters.

The boat slid off the tree with a large splash. The roots had disengaged themselves as the craft had rocked from side to side during the fight. Most of the money was gone. Gregor's temper flared. Only four canvas duffels were left.

He had to get off the river and onto shore before they lost any more. Between him and Johnson, they could steer the boat. They had to. He had a plane to catch.

Chapter Sixteen

Marcus piloted the boat through trees, brush and debris to the gravel landing. The caretaker's cabin was straight ahead. As soon as he found a phone and Cally was safe, he was leaving to stop Gregor on his own. His rule-book professionalism was in tatters.

They were racing toward doing something they'd both regret later. Well, he wouldn't regret it, but Cally would. He had to protect her, even from himself at this point, if he could.

He hoped he was strong enough.

Ten minutes later she was helping him break the glass out of Mr. Sydney's kitchen window.

"Where do you suppose he is? Grocery shopping?" Marcus's words were sharper than he intended when he opened the door.

Cally was shivering; she shrugged into a jacket she found at the entrance. "The telephone is right through there." She pointed to the living area and went to look for dry clothes.

The room was spartanly furnished, dominated by a Franklin stove with a worn vinyl recliner and a television set. Along the walls were numerous fly rods interspersed among the stuffed trophies.

The entire place smelled of fried fish and wood smoke. He didn't mind the odor, especially when he spied the gun cabinet in the corner. Two shotguns, three rifles and several handguns; Sydney was well-outfitted for his job—or a small military coup.

"I've found clothes," she called from the other room and wandered back in with an armful of sweatpants and shirts.

"Why don't you take a shower? It'll warm you up. Your teeth are chattering. I'm going to be a few minutes on the phone."

She froze in the process of pulling on another sweater. "What about Harris?"

There was no way to sugarcoat this. "Trust me. I've got to call in. Asa knows what's going on. Hopefully, he's already talked to Hodges. But in case he hasn't, I've got to."

"But what if…"

"Cally, there's nothing to gain by not calling at this point. Gregor may have capsized out there. If that's the case, we need help to find your boy."

"You think he's already dead, don't you?" Her voice was hollow.

Marcus put down the phone, hesitating only a moment before wrapping his arms around her. The sweater she'd picked was huge and smelled like a campfire. Her hair was still wet against his shoulder. He felt the tension in her body but wasn't sure if it was from her agitation or his embrace.

"No, I don't think he's dead. But I do think Gregor's got him somewhere. Maybe they've got him staying with someone—a friend of Gregor's or of one of the other men. We'll find him, but we've got to have help. The sooner the better."

"Why can't we wait?" Her words were muffled against his chest.

"Because if Gregor did capsize on the river, he's not going to call the person with Harris. That individual won't know what to do with the boy. If the boat didn't capsize, Gregor's plans are at the very least seriously…screwed. He'll be more concerned about getting out of town than getting your son."

She relaxed against him. God, he must be seriously depraved—but he just wanted to hold her like this a little longer.

She lifted her head from his chest. "Your boss's men will be careful, right…they wouldn't shoot him or anything until we know about Harris? They won't do anything stupid like that, will they?"

"No. No, they won't. Trust me." Marcus hoped like hell he was right.

He studied her eyes. Her nose was red and her chin was scraped but her eyes were dry. He reached out to touch her cheek.

"Could you hold me a little longer?"

He tightened his arms around her; she tucked her chin into his chest.

"Thank you," she whispered.

Marcus laughed softly, "This is not exactly a hardship."

He looked down at her worrying that lower lip, felt her heart beating against his and he wanted her.

He'd lied earlier by the river. Kissing her had meant more than God-I'm-glad-to-be-alive. She made him want things he hadn't thought were possible anymore. He was leaning toward her to kiss her again when she took a deep breath and slipped out of his arms.

"I know you're right. Make the call." She walked away into a bathroom that opened off the living area.

Thank God, she was smarter than he was. He stared hard at the door until he heard the shower start, then he dialed the phone.

It had been two hours since the robbery and Hodges had already gotten word of the explosion through channels since his men were part of the special task force in that area. He was on his way from Jackson and tried to chew Marcus out for not calling sooner, but the connection was so bad, the lieutenant finally gave up and they stuck to essentials.

Harris's kidnapping. The robbery. The river.

Marcus held the line while Hodges barked orders to someone else about getting out an AMBER Alert, then Hodges was back explaining that Asa had been the person in the headlights at the Paddlewheel landing before the generator explosion. He was badly burned and in the emergency room in Murphy's Point. Marcus could hear Hodges talking to someone in the background.

"The task force should be on-site in an hour. You wait for them," said Hodges. "Right now, the local authorities are in charge. They've been tied up at some factory fire. The whole damn county is there. Took us forever to find the sheriff."

With the static-filled connection, Marcus caught every other word, but Hodges's frustration with local law enforcement came through loud and clear.

"They blew up the bridge on River Road so it took a while before emergency vehicles were able to get to the casino. Some brilliant soul finally realized that they could just drive through the fields around the culvert. We've got a couple of choppers on the way. They'll start the search on the river."

"The boat we were in practically capsized. I don't know if those guys are still out there or not. They could have drowned by now for all I know," said Marcus.

"We can only hope."

Marcus was grateful Cally hadn't heard that. "How fast will that AMBER Alert go out from your chopper?"

"It's happening as we speak. The FBI will probably want to send a team in, as well. We've got the ball rolling now."

It wasn't much, but given the circumstances, it was all they could do.

"There's an injured man at River Trace," Marcus continued. Hodges got on another phone to get an ambulance to the bed-and-breakfast and Marcus held the line again.

"Lieutenant, I'll meet you at the airstrip. That's where Gregor was planning to meet his pilot."

"You watch your ass. And you wait for backup, Marcus. An hour…that's all it will take for someone to reach you, but you wait. That's an order. I'm not losing anyone else tonight.

"Yes, sir."

The shower was still running when Marcus hung up with an hour to kill.

He stared at the gun cabinet. He'd like to get into it without having to break it to pieces, if possible. He was still studying the problem when Cally emerged from the bathroom wrapped in a threadbare towel.

Steam rolled out of the doorway behind her and wet curls rioted around her face. Her skin was flushed from the heat. His body's instinctive response was immediate.

Part of him wanted to finish what they'd started at the river. But keeping Cally safe was more important than anything he wanted. And the only way to keep her safe was to ignore what the lizard part of his brain craved.

"Any word on Harris?" Her voice was hopeful.

He hated watching her face fall as he shook his head. "Cally, it's going to be okay."

She nodded but started biting that lower lip. He wasn't sure he could have this conversation with her barely dressed and not touch her. The memory of what had happened earlier was too fresh on his mind.

"No news isn't necessarily a bad thing in this case, right?" she asked.

"That's right." He was distinctly uncomfortable with lying to her, but this was what she needed to hear—a lie for her sanity's sake. No news was *not* good news. But she didn't need to know that now. *Do whatever it takes to keep the civilian calm.* "It's okay."

She nodded once and tried to smile, but two large tears formed at the corners of her eyes.

"No, it's not okay. You're just saying that. I understand why. I'm sorry I'm such a mess, and that you think you have to lie to me to keep me from flipping out. I—"

Once she started crying, it was over. All sense of professionalism was just...gone. There was no way he could keep this impersonal.

"It's gonna be all right," he whispered. He hesitated for a moment, but she didn't seem to notice.

He couldn't turn away from her. That would be cruel. So he did what he really wanted to do—he pulled her into his arms. She began to cry in earnest.

"I know this is difficult. And you're being so strong. So brave. You're going to survive this. No, not hearing isn't great, but it's not horrible, either. Just hang on."

And hang on she did. Melting into his arms, she didn't seem to care that he was covered in the river water she'd just washed off herself. Her tears were hot on his skin. The sobs were deep, racking her body. But she clung to him and wept, hard.

He held her close as she cried, rubbing his palms up and down her back, extraordinarily careful to keep his hands on the ragged terry cloth, knowing he couldn't have her.

Not like this. Not now. Not while she was frantic over her son. Marcus's timing was forever abysmal.

He murmured comforting words into her hair; she gave a shuddering breath but didn't raise her head. Slowly her tears subsided, and when she finally quieted and looked up at him, his hand stilled at her waist.

Her nose was red and her eyes were puffy, but she was studying him with an intensity that had him rethinking his choice earlier about not touching her skin. The look in her eyes now wasn't about fear or grief. And it wasn't cool the way it had been in the nursery Sunday night. Her gaze now was all about need and want.

He stared hard to make sure he wasn't misreading anything as he had then. She started to slide her arms from around his waist, and he took a deep breath.

Good, this wasn't going to happen. Because he wasn't going to be able to tell her *no* if she turned it into something else.

He didn't want to say *no*.

The part of him that had wanted her the first night he saw

her opening the door of River Trace—the same part of him that hadn't wanted to pull away when she'd tried to seduce him in the nursery, even after he knew it was all about getting her son back—that part of him was still all about finishing what they'd started.

But nothing was going to happen, and he was relieved because he wasn't going to be able to stop himself if she pushed him.

Then the world slipped sideways.

She stepped back and reached for the towel at her breast, tilting her chin up a notch. He stopped her before she could loosen the knot.

"Are you sure?" He felt a little foolish asking because it was pretty obvious she was sure.

"I need you to help me forget about this for a while."

He shook his head and put his hand over hers to stall her.

"I know what I want," she insisted, staring deep into his eyes. It was as if she could see everything inside him, and he couldn't hide, even though she was the one who was about to be exposed.

This was not how he wanted it to happen.

"I don't want you to regret doing this," he explained.

"That's the least of my worries. Are you concerned *you'll* regret it?" She raised an eyebrow and whisked away the towel…and there was nothing more for him to say.

He could only stare, speechless for a moment at the lush expanse of creamy skin. She was all full breasts and rounded hips, perfect in his mind. Marcus was out of strength, resolve and willpower to walk away.

He quit thinking about doing anything by the book and reached for her. As she bumped into his hips with her stomach, there was no way she could miss that he wanted her. He took a step back, but she reached for him instead.

She pulled him closer and slid one hand between them to fumble with his zipper. Any thought he'd had of walking away died when she slipped her hand inside his jeans. He crushed his mouth to hers and filled his hands with her, pulling away only to carry her to the bedroom.

The bedspread was a blanket and smelled faintly of wood smoke, but he didn't care as long as Cally was in the middle of it. She pulled at his damp clothes and kissed her way across his chest and down his abdomen.

When she would have traveled further south, he reached for her hips and turned her on her back. Her eyes widened but she smiled softly as he pushed his way inside her.

She murmured things he couldn't understand, but they didn't matter when she wrapped her legs around him. Then it was just his body against hers.

Her skin was silky smooth and he inhaled the scent of shampoo, soap and woman as she climaxed before him, pressing her hands into his chest. He leaned down to kiss her again, pushing deeper, then he rose over her one last time, shuddering his own release while he whispered her name.

HE STARED into Cally's face. Her lips were red and swollen from his kisses; her eyes were starting to focus on him, changing from dreamy to clear. He wasn't sure he wanted to know what she was thinking.

He knew she was going to be sorry. She was going to regret having sex with him. He just didn't know when.

He was still over her, balanced on an elbow and breathing hard when the sound of a plane, flying low, registered. It was making a second pass when Marcus recognized the sound for what it was.

"Marcus, I—"

"That's Gregor's plane. It has to be."

"Oh, then we have to go," she wriggled underneath him. His body's response was not exactly what he was expecting. His head was still spinning as she scrambled from the bed to throw on clothes. He should've been moving right along with her, but he could only stare.

"We'll have to hurry." She pulled on a loud pink T-shirt with no bra and faded jeans. "Why aren't you moving?"

He grinned. "I'm just admiring the scenery."

She threw sweatpants and a T-shirt at his head. "Come on, move it."

"Where'd you get your clean clothes?"

"Sydney has lady friends who sleep over."

"You know an awful lot about Sydney." He tugged on the borrowed sweats.

"Yeah. We're buddies."

He wondered what that meant while he pulled on his appropriated clothes and filled her in on the conversation with Hodges. They went to the living room for shoes. She'd found some boots that almost fit her, belonging to one of Sydney's women friends.

"You know so much about Sydney. Do you know how to get into that gun case without destroying it?"

"Sure." She reached behind the cabinet and produced a small cylindrical key.

Marcus raised an eyebrow. "Buddies, huh?"

"He and Jamie hunted together a lot."

She unlocked the door to pull a .270 deer rifle and a revolver from the case. In the drawer below, she rummaged for ammunition. Marcus's gun was somewhere at the bottom of the Mississippi. She pulled a holster from the cabinet and slipped it around her own waist.

"What are you doing?" He asked.

"I'm going with you." She stopped to look at him.

"That's crazy."

"You're right. All of this is completely insane."

He was fairly certain she was including what they'd just done in the bedroom, as well.

"But you don't even know where you are, so I'm coming too. You'll have to trust me. Just like I'm trusting you to ge

Harris back. Do you have any idea how hard it is for me to do that? To let someone else be in control? I haven't trusted anyone to take care of us since Jamie died. So you have to let me come with you. You gonna be okay with that?"

Chapter Seventeen

Marcus wasn't okay with it, but they were back on the water anyway. Cally had refused to stay at Sydney's cabin and they didn't have time to argue. The plane had landed early.

He hated waiting on backup. But since Cally was with him, he didn't have much choice. They could at least take a look from a hidden corner of the field.

It was almost 6:00 a.m. The sun would be up soon—a sliver of pink had appeared on the horizon and was getting brighter by the minute. Growing morning light made it easier to see the bank and debris the boat could snag on.

He spotted the field and a nosed-over plane. Cally had been right about the airstrip. He steered toward a vine-covered elm. He was about to jump out of the boat when she caught his arm.

"Snakes," she warned, pointing at the base of the tree.

Peering through the brush where he'd been about to step, he spied the bed of moccasins. Their fat bodies were wrapped around the tree's roots and each other like a bowl of writhing brown pasta.

"Damn."

Focused on the plane, he hadn't been paying attention. He backed the boat out to motor further down the shoreline. This time he carefully checked before stepping onto the muddy bank.

"Any chance you'll stay put?" he asked.

She shook her head and scrambled up the bank behind him, mud sucking at her borrowed boots. They crept toward the downed plane.

Had anyone even survived that? He had to check, orders or no.

The sun was barely over the horizon; long shadows criss-crossed the field. The Cessna rested on its nose and left wing like a child's toy that had been discarded in a fit of temper. The propeller had snapped off and lay a hundred yards away.

They were almost to the door when a gruff voice boomed out of the shadows. "Who the hell are you?"

Marcus froze. A burly man with a 12-gauge stood beside the cockpit. He was outfitted for the invasion of a small country or opening day of hunting season, however one chose to look at it. Wearing a camouflage jacket and pants with an ammo belt across his shoulder, he appeared to be around seventy years old. He carried a large hunting knife on his belt as well as a .357 Magnum.

"Hello, Mr. Sydney. It's me, Cally Burnett." Marcus jumped as Cally shouted a greeting.

Ignoring the 12-gauge, she strode past Marcus to give the camo-attired giant a hug.

"Cally Burnett, what in the world are you doing out here?" The man's voice was unnaturally loud and he glared at Marcus over the top of her head. "What's that guy doing with my .270?"

Marcus looked at the gun in his hands, still recovering from the shock of seeing Cally walk into the embrace of an armed man.

"It's a terribly long story, Mr. Sydney. We had to borrow it, and I'm afraid we broke your kitchen window."

Mr. Sydney seemed to take her explanation—or rather, lack of one—in stride with no questions. She was still shouting despite her proximity to him.

"Who've you got in there?" Cally pointed toward the plane.

"I don't rightly know. Ain't a member, that's for sure." Sydney led them to a man in a camouflage flight suit lying unconscious on the other side of the downed Cessna.

While his back was to her, Cally whispered, "Sydney's a little deaf."

"I figured that out," said Marcus.

Unable to hear them, Sydney was still talking. "...all know you can't land on this field right now with the water like it is."

He eyed Marcus as he continued, "I just got here myself. The fellow was conscious when I put my head through the door, but he passed out when I was getting him out of the plane. He's pretty banged-up."

Marcus knelt beside the pilot Gregor had bragged about— Calvin Renfro. At least, that's who he assumed this was. His face was a mess, with a broken nose and deep gashes on his forehead along with a huge goose egg.

Marcus hoped there wasn't a neck injury. He checked; the man's pulse was strong and steady, so it was probably just a concussion. He studied the plane. Renfro was extremely lucky.

"Now who are you exactly?" Sydney boomed.

"A cop," said Marcus, raising his voice. "This man was here to pick up men who robbed the Paddlewheel tonight."

"Humph," said Sydney. "Where are they?"

"No idea. If they're coming, they should be here any time now."

"How about we get over in that deer stand and wait for 'em?" Sydney pointed to the wooden shed atop the seven-foot pilings at the edge of the field.

Marcus considered the idea. *Why not?*

If Gregor showed, he wasn't going anywhere and Cally would be out of their way. If they didn't show, it looked like as good a place as any to wait for the task force. According to Hodges, their chopper should be along anytime now.

"All right, lead the way, Sydney."

"What about this fellow?"

"Well, there's not much we can do for him until we get medical help here. We shouldn't move him any more. I'll stay behind with him just in case."

"Whatever," Sydney shrugged. An uncomplicated guy, he tromped away, leading Cally toward the deer stand.

"THAT GUY'S a damn cop. He was playing us the whole freakin' time!" Johnson's curses colored the air.

Gregor walked beside him, thinking the same thing. They'd hidden on the other side of the field and heard the entire exchange between Cally, Marcus and Sydney.

Gregor didn't say a word. Johnson was quietly raving enough for the both of them. He carried the three canvas bags. Gregor's broken arm was in a makeshift splint and sling; he carried only one duffel.

"We're screwed, aren't we?" asked Johnson.

"No, not yet, damn it. But shut up. I've got to think for a minute."

They made their way back to the boat and tossed the canvas bags in next to Boggs, who was still unconscious. They'd shored up just down from an elm tree. Johnson was still mumbling as he untied the boat, not paying attention to what he was doing.

He stepped right in the middle of a bed of water moccasins.

True to their aggressive nature, the cottonmouths immediately struck at him—their mouths flashing white just before their fangs sank into his legs. It was like something out of a horror movie.

Two of them wrapped around his ankles, biting repeatedly. He was screaming as Gregor tried to pull him away from the tree with his good arm. Three of the snakes followed for several yards.

"Shoot 'em. Get 'em off me. They're biting. Gregor, help me!" Urine ran down Johnson's leg as he kicked and backed away.

Gregor used his silenced revolver to shoot the cottonmouths not attached to Johnson's body. Three dying snakes writhed on the ground while the other two around his ankles slithered off.

Johnson was crying and babbling by the time the reptiles disappeared into the brush. "Oh, Jesus, they bit me. I'm gonna die. What am I gonna do?"

Gregor took off his belt and made a tourniquet at the top of Johnson's leg, an arduous process with only one hand.

"Rob, you've got to lie still. That way the venom won't work as quickly. The snakes are gone now. Try to stay calm."

"But those were cottonmouths, man. I'm gonna die, aren't I?"

Gregor didn't answer. He just kept working on the tourniquet. When he finished, he studied Johnson. The man's breathing had slowed, but Gregor wasn't sure if he was calming down or if the poison was already taking effect. He had to think fast, and Johnson wasn't going to like any of his ideas.

"You need immediate medical attention. The best thing I can do for you is leave you here—"

"What do you mean, leave me?"

"Marcus and that other man heard you shouting. They're probably on their way right now. They can help you. I can't. I don't have any kind of first aid to offer." Gregor stood.

"You sorry SOB! You're just gonna leave me? You're worse than Boggs." He tried to stand but couldn't. The venom was definitely doing its thing.

Gregor didn't answer and began walking back toward the boat, keeping an eye out for other snakes.

"You bastard," shouted Johnson. "I'll get you, if it's the last thing I do."

Gregor didn't slow down.

"I'll tell them everything—where you're going, how you're getting there."

Gregor stopped. *That would never do.* He pulled the .38 from his holster before he turned around.

"I can't believe you'd leave me, man. After all that brotherhood crap you've shoveled down our throats about the company."

Johnson's wild eyes were glazed and unfocused as he spat the words. Spittle clung to one corner of his mouth. He didn't see the gun when Gregor moved toward him. "I'll tell them everything they want to know. Everything—"

The shot went straight through Johnson's heart. He was dead before his head hit the ground. The expression on his angry face never changed.

Gregor told himself that the man was already dead from the snake bites anyway. He'd just hurried the process along. Done him a favor, really. Less painful in the long run.

He slipped the gun into his shoulder holster, but he couldn't fasten the safety strap with the sling in the way. When he shoved the boat away from the bank to jump in, the revolver slipped from the leather case and splashed into the river.

Damn! What an idiotic thing to do. Now he'd have to find another weapon. He contemplated looking for it in the water. It wasn't deep, but seeing a snake wrapped around the branch of a nearby tree made him think better of that idea.

He looked at the four bags piled in the middle of the boat and the man lying beside them. Boggs's head still oozed blood but his breathing seemed normal. Gregor pulled away from the shore and stopped. He hesitated only a moment.

No. More. Splits.

With a grunt and a shove he heaved Boggs over the side. There was a loud splash, then nothing as the body sank into the shallow water.

The man probably had brain damage anyway. Gregor was doing him a favor. He shook his head and started the motor.

The tree roots had sheared off two propeller blades, severely crippling the boat. His arm hurt like a son of a bitch and he was going to have to use a paddle. But he could do it.

The alternate escape plan was his only option now. Plus, he had a score to settle. Hate would keep him going like nothing else could.

BY THE TIME they found Johnson's body, the sun was filtering through the trees with few shadows left.

"Lordy mercy, would you look at that," said Sydney.

"Oh my God!" Cally paled and turned away.

Marcus *was* looking and could hardly believe his eyes. Rob Johnson lay flat on his back with a belt wrapped around his leg and three dead water moccasins stretched out beside his body. Bloodstains streaked his ripped pants in multiple places below the knee where he assumed the snakes' fangs had gouged the flesh.

Marcus quit counting bites when he reached eleven. They were so startling, he almost missed the bullet hole in Johnson's chest. There was little blood and the bullet wound appeared insignificant compared to the bites, even though that shot was obviously the coup de grâce.

"I ain't never seen nothin' like that in all my born days," said Sydney. "Why, he musta' stepped into a den of 'em."

"Yeah." Marcus flashed on his narrow escape of the same fate, then blocked out the caretaker's running commentary as he puzzled over what could have happened to Johnson.

He hadn't heard any shots after the man's shouts. Of course, Sydney hadn't even heard the shouts. But he and Cally had seen Marcus running toward the far end of the field and come barreling after him.

"I think it's safe to assume the men either saw the downed plane, heard our conversation with Sydney, or both."

Cally nodded but didn't look back at Johnson's body. Sydney couldn't hear him. He was still marveling over the snake bites.

"Even if Sams survived on the river, he's in no shape to help them. That leaves only Gregor and Boggs. Now they know you and I are alive and that I'm a cop."

"Why shoot Johnson?" asked Cally.

He looked at the snakes again and felt the bile rise in back of his throat. "Given the option of dying from multiple cottonmouth bites or a simple bullet through the heart, I'd prefer a bullet."

Sydney walked around the body. "I wouldn't wish the moccasins on my worst enemy."

Cally shuddered.

"Gregor is probably the one who shot him. Boggs isn't cold-blooded enough. Boggs could stand back and watch someone die, but I don't think he could kill them outright."

He wished the words back as soon as he spoke them because they only served to ratchet up Cally's anxiety level.

"What about Harris? Where do you think Gregor's headed now?" she asked.

"My best guess would be across the river into Louisiana. He has to know the authorities will be searching for him soon. More than likely he'll try to ditch the boat and get a car."

"But where?" Her voice rose with the strain of all she'd seen in the past few hours. "They can't hurt him, he's our only link to Harris. We've got to find Gregor."

The sound of a helicopter floated over the water.

"I know." Marcus reached for her hand. Her fingers were ice-cold; her eyes were filled with that same gut-wrenching fear he'd seen out on the water.

"What are you going to do to find him?"

He rubbed her palms between his own. "The cavalry just arrived. If Gregor's on the river, we'll find him."

He didn't say what he was thinking, even though it was the one bright spot about this whole scenario having gone tits up. Gregor wasn't going to have time to deal with taking his revenge on Cally, Marcus or Harris. He was going to be too busy saving his own ass.

Chapter Eighteen

At the airstrip, a helicopter had landed at the far end of the field on stable ground. Men were already taking care of Calvin Renfro. Marcus held on to Cally's hand when the officer directed him to a radio; he was patched through to Hodges.

The headset they gave him made it impossible for her to hear both sides of the conversation. The connection wasn't much better than the one they'd had earlier. Marcus explained what he'd found.

Hodges's reply was full of static. They'd put him on a chopper in Natchez to come to Palmers.

"I'm sure you're right and Gregor is long gone, but we'll have to search the hunting camp anyway. I'll get some men out there with a K-9 unit. They'll check across the river on the Louisiana side, as well. Damn. This is gonna get crazy with all the jurisdictional crap. But we need the help. It's a tremendous area to cover."

"What about the boy?" Marcus asked. Cally squeezed his hand and he looked down to meet her worried gaze.

Watching her was too distracting. He had to turn away even as he tightened his grip. He couldn't forget how she'd looked into his eyes just before they'd made love. It was as though she could see all of him, even the parts of himself he'd been keeping hidden away.

"Nothing yet. The FBI's sending a team up later this morning. I'm still hoping Asa can help us when he comes to."

"What's the latest? How's he doing?"

"Fair. They're 'careflighting' him to the burn unit in Jackson as soon as he stabilizes. Burns are over twenty percent of his body. Legs and arms mostly. He hasn't regained consciousness since they found him. The doctors say he'll survive but will need extensive skin grafts."

Marcus cringed at the pain his partner had yet to endure.

"What about Kevin Tucker?"

"He'll be all right, barring any complications. You and Bay Wiggins did some good doctoring there. McCay County deputies are at the bed-and-breakfast securing the scene."

"You okay with that?" asked Marcus.

"It's not like I've got a hell of a lot of choice. Who knows? Maybe they'll turn up something about the kid."

Marcus heard the exasperation in Hodges's voice and practically read his thoughts. Those deputies might turn up evidence about Harris. But with all those people tromping through the house, it was doubtful.

It was more likely the county would screw up the scene before the task force and crime-scene technicians got there. Marcus had seen it happen more times than he cared to count. The bottom line was Hodges didn't have enough people to cover all the bases, so he was going to have to trust local law enforcement.

"We should be there within the next thirty minutes." Hodges signed off and Marcus gave Cally the news.

"Kevin is going to be all right. They've got officers swarming all over your house right now."

"What about Harris?" There was hope in her voice but not her eyes.

Marcus shook his head. "Nothing yet."

LIEUTENANT HODGES landed at Palmers twenty-five minutes later with a group of camo-attired officers wearing Kevlar vests and headsets similar to those Cally had seen on Gregor and his men.

Hodges introduced himself, assuring her that everything possible was being done to find Harris. He took Marcus aside and she watched from a distance as they talked. She couldn't hear what was being said, but quite a bit of non-verbal communication was going on. Obviously, Hodges was reading Marcus the riot act now that he had him face to face.

Marcus had told her about the task force while they were swimming into shore on their "breaks." Hodges would also take a lot of heat for Marcus not reporting Gregor's plans earlier. Would the gamble Marcus had taken pay off?

After his spirited conversation with the lieutenant, Marcus hustled Cally onto the helicopter with Renfro, the downed pilot.

"Where are we going?" she shouted as the chopper lifted off the ground. He pointed to a squad car and an ambulance waiting for them on the other side of the levee.

"The squad car is taking you back to River Trace. I'm catching a ride in the ambulance with Renfro to see if I can talk to Asa before he's transferred to the burn unit in Jackson."

The chopper landed almost immediately. She felt rather than heard the gravel crunching under her feet. The screaming engines drowned out all other noise as Marcus walked her toward the police car.

She didn't want to leave him. She needed to tell him…so many things. To thank him for saving her. For risking his job, his life. For everything. To tell him to be careful.

Medical personnel hustled around Renfro, loading him into the EMT van.

"Trust me, Cally."

She held onto his sleeve. "I…"

Everything she wanted to say ran through her head in a jumble. *I care for you. I'm scared for you. Be careful.*

What came out was: "I'm trying to trust you…to believe you'll get him back. I hate feeling so powerless."

Damn. Not what she'd meant to say at all.

"I'll call you after I see Asa. He may be able to tell us something."

She nodded woodenly, trying to steel herself against the growing despair. He touched her hand and she went to him, wrapping herself in his arms. She'd taken him by surprise. She could tell by the look in his eyes.

Shaken herself, she tilted her head up to kiss him—channeling all the desperation and need she felt into this moment. To really trust him meant letting go. It scared her more than anything she'd faced so far.

The kiss was entirely different from what they'd shared in Sydney's cabin. She pulled away first. "Find him," she whispered.

He nodded and handed her into the passenger seat. He leaned in, staring into her eyes a final time before he touched her face. There was nothing left to say.

Closing the door, he waited until her car was driving away before he climbed into the ambulance.

EXHAUSTION overwhelmed Cally as the squad car drove away from River Trace. Standing on the front steps, she felt like she'd been away for days rather than hours. She rang the doorbell, and, a moment later, Luella was wrapping her in a big hug.

"Oh, honey. We've been so worried." She patted Cally's shoulder, trying to soothe, "It's gonna be okay, sweetheart. You're home. It's gonna be all right."

Only if they find Harris. Dry-eyed, Cally gently pulled away from the embrace, determined to control the one thing she had left, her emotions. Her stomach twisted as she watched Luella cry—sniffling and wiping her eyes with an apron.

Now it was Cally's turn to pat the older woman's back. She longed to say something that would give them both courage. Unfortunately, she felt woefully inadequate.

"I know they're going to find him, Lu. I'm sure of it." Her voice was strong, if a bit thick. She let out a ragged sigh.

Luella blew her nose and nodded. "The police were here earlier. Looking upstairs at the rooms where those men were staying. There's tape across the doors and we aren't supposed to go in them. The officers said they'd be back later."

"Where's Bay?"

"Out in the kitchen. We've been cleaning up after…after Kevin."

Cally nodded. "They told Marcus he's going to be fine. He's at the hospital in Murphy's Point. I'll get changed and go in later to check on him. Do you think they've called Roger? I suppose I could do that—"

She was prattling and stopped abruptly. Luella hadn't asked her about Marcus, about Harris, about anything. Cally knew her friend must have a million questions about all of it. Things must look horribly grim for her not to be pressing for answers.

"I think I'll go take a shower. Would you bring me some hot tea, please?"

"Sure, honey. You want anything else? Maybe a little something to eat?"

"No, not right now, Luella. Thanks. Maybe later."

She stopped to talk with Bay on her way through the kitchen. He was on his hands and knees with a scrub brush and bucket. She could smell the bleach he was using to remove the bloodstains from the grout. The scent made her queasy.

He wiped his hands on a rag and stood when she walked in. "Harris is gonna be all right, Cally. You hold on to that."

"I am, Bay. I am." She was feeling stronger. She could do this. "You don't have to clean that. I'll do it after I shower. You must be tired." She started toward her bedroom.

"No, ma'am. I'll take care of it."

Cally stopped, remembering those same words.

Was it just two mornings ago? Harris's fish.

She turned back to gaze at Bay. The words had registered

with him, as well. She could see it in his eyes. At that moment she became incredibly nauseated.

Oh God, she mustn't do this to herself. She had to hold it together—just a little longer. She swallowed as she felt her stomach lurch.

"Thank you," she managed. "I appreciate that and...everything you and Luella have done. I'm going to go get cleaned up now. I'll be back in a bit."

She made it to the bathroom before she threw up and turned the shower on so they couldn't hear her retching. Afterward, she slowly stripped off her borrowed clothes and climbed under the hot, soothing spray. Seated on the shower floor, she leaned her head back against the tile and wept until she was completely spent.

Too tired to cry anymore, she watched the steam float around her. *Oh, Harris baby, hang on...I love you...Marcus is trying to find you.* She lost track of time as the water gradually turned cooler.

Standing up with a short burst of energy, she made it out just before the water turned to ice. Surprisingly, she felt better. Tired and wrung-out, but better, all the same.

She put on a robe and dabbed antiseptic ointment on the multitude of scratches on her arms and legs. She couldn't remember where they had come from, probably the debris in the river. She combed the tangles out of her hair on autopilot but struggled to keep her eyes open.

Dazed from her emotional meltdown, she wandered into the bedroom. Looking around she realized how thoroughly Luella and Bay been had been cleaning. There was no sign that a man with a gunshot wound had spent the night here. The freshly made bed beckoned to her exhausted body. On the nightstand, a steaming cup of peppermint tea perfumed the air.

I'll lie down for a few minutes. Then I'll go see about Kevin...and Harris.

She pulled back the covers to crawl in. The linens felt cool against her cheek.

If I could stop thinking for just a few minutes and close my eyes for a bit...

She drifted off to sleep as the tea cooled.

Chapter Nineteen

Marcus hurried down the hall of McCay County Medical Center. Asa's private room was next to the ICU; he appeared to be sleeping, his face covered with white cream and yards of gauze.

The nurse said he'd regained consciousness thirty minutes earlier, but they'd just given him an injection for pain. The translation being, "Don't expect much."

Asa's green eyes fluttered open. "Hey, look what the cat drug in."

"Hey, yourself, man. How you feeling?"

"How do I look?" Asa's whispering voice sounded rustier than usual. Smoke from the explosion had gotten into his lungs.

Marcus stared at the bits of red skin showing through the gauze and cream. Asa's shoulders were uncovered. Scrapes and scratches blanketed his chest. His left arm was wrapped in gauze; two IVs ran in the vicinity of his right wrist.

"Like hell?" he offered.

Asa barked a laugh that became a coughing fit. Marcus found the straw-topped container of water next to the bed, and Asa drank deeply.

"Yeah. That's pretty much how I feel. Doc says I'll be my usual handsome self in no time."

Marcus laughed, grateful for his partner's sense of humor. He was going to need it in the coming days.

"Could I have more water?" Asa's lids drifted shut.

Marcus directed the straw to his friend's lips. "Why did you follow us to the river?"

Asa's eyes snapped open. "I had to tell you. I found the boy."

Marcus bobbled the big cup getting it back to the table. "Where?"

"He's at Earleen and Manny's."

"What? You're not joking, are you?"

"Swear to God. I saw Manny in the casino and he told me Earleen was 'babysitting' for Frank and Carlotta. I knew it had to be your kid."

"You're sure he's there?"

Asa's eyes drifted closed again. "As sure as I can be. The phones weren't working by the time I found out, but who else could it be?"

Marcus could tell he was hurting, but his voice grew stronger as he talked.

"Well, let me call her," said Marcus. "She's gotta be freaked out by now. There's an AMBER Alert out for him."

"Ah geez, I hope she doesn't rabbit. Surely she's got enough sense to call you if she sees something like that on TV?"

Marcus picked up the hospital phone. "It's not that calling the police would be bad for Harris, but she had nothing to do with the robbery. She just has bad friends. I don't want her mixed up in this."

He tried Earleen at home.

No answer. Same thing when he tried her cell.

His own hadn't survived the swim in the river, so he had to go through the laborious process of accessing his voice mail through Asa's hospital line.

Ten minutes later, cussing, he'd retrieved the messages. He filled Asa in on everything that had happened after the casino as he slogged through seven howling voice mails from Hodges. Then there was Earleen's deep congested voice.

"Marcus, it's me. I think I'm in trouble and I'm scared. Call me, please. I'm at the Dew Drop Inn in Vidalia." She rattled off a phone number. "I'm not answering my cell anymore. It's about Frank and Carlotta."

Marcus couldn't believe it might be this easy. He dialed the number and she answered on the first ring.

"Earleen?" A child was crying in the background and his heart lurched.

"Marcus, thank God you called. I'm in a world of hurt. Carlotta and Frank completely screwed me over. I had no idea they'd—"

"It's okay. I know everything."

There was a long silence punctuated by Harris's sobs. "Is the boy okay?"

"I don't know. He's been crying for his mama since Carlotta dropped him with me. But he doesn't have fever or anything. I think he's just real upset."

As well he should be, thought Marcus.

"I swear, I had no idea they'd kidnapped him."

"I believe you."

"You've always believed me, when no one else would have."

"We all need someone to believe in us, Earleen. Everyone screws up sometime."

He didn't trust himself to say any more sitting beside his injured partner, but he held on to what she'd said. The affirmation that he'd absolutely made the right call all those years ago on Farish Street.

"You trusting me to go home on that bus made a difference whether you realized it or not."

He swallowed the lump in his throat. "Okay. Here's what's doing. I'm coming to get the boy. We're not going to traumatize him any further with lots of police and such. You just sit tight, and I'll be there as soon as possible. Got it?"

"Okay. We're in Room 207. Second floor, back around by the pool. I'm not answering the door 'less it's you." *Click.*

Marcus stared at the phone for a minute.

"Told you so," Asa slurred.

"Yeah, you did. I gotta go get him. Cally's been going out of her mind."

"Yeah, sure." He was obviously struggling to focus. "One more thing I've got to tell you. It's important."

Marcus stopped on his way to the door.

"I know you've had a ration of crap from the department since everything went down last fall, and I...I wanted to say thank you."

"Man. You don't have to—" Marcus so did not want to hear this.

"Yeah. Yeah, I do. We've never talked about it and you've never asked me but...I took the money."

Marcus couldn't speak as Asa struggled with the difficult words and the painkillers. "It was after they'd taken you to the hospital. I went back to Donny's after. Everyone had gone home and I found the cash. No one knew it was there. The evidence guys missed it."

Marcus let him go on, but he didn't really want to. He'd already figured this out a while back, and it was uncomfortable to hear his friend's confession.

"The cash was in the television set—taped over. You've been covering for me, but I did it. We needed the money for Trey's therapy. The bills were past due, and insurance wasn't going to pay for any more rehab. I want my boy to walk again."

Asa sighed. His breathing was labored. "I justified it to myself by saying it was drug money, and it wasn't going to do anything but sit in an evidence locker. I'm sorry."

Marcus shook his head. No way was he going to throw the first stone. Not after Tessa and all of his own colossal failures.

With what Asa had just told him, his partner could be sent to prison. At that moment Marcus made his decision. When this was over he would resign.

The job wasn't worth it. He'd never reveal what Asa had just confessed. It made him tired even to think about it.

Tessa. Who he'd become working undercover. What he'd

caught a glimpse of with Cally and Harris before their world went mad. He wanted…things that probably weren't possible.

"Asa, don't say another word. Please."

"I have to say thank you for covering for me." His words slurred again. "I know it's put your career in the toilet. I'm sorry for that. I let you down. But I didn't know what else to do to pro—"

Marcus couldn't stand to hear Asa beat himself up. "It's all right. If you only knew what I'd—"

"No," Asa interrupted. "It's not all right. Not really. But I'd do it again, anyway. Given my other options. For my family. My son. You do what's necessary…" Asa's voice drifted off as he fell asleep.

Marcus looked down at his partner. He'd explain later. When he'd made it right. "I would, too," he murmured.

Asa didn't respond.

Marcus took his right hand and squeezed it. "Get well, my friend."

MARCUS BORROWED a phone from the Natchez police officer now waiting outside Asa's room. They were having a vigil even though Asa wasn't one of their own. Marcus wandered down the hall for privacy. He was about to open a whole new jurisdictional can of worms.

A Mississippi kidnap victim being recovered in Louisiana. Everybody would want in on that one. He wanted to be there himself.

Not because he wanted the glory, but because it would scare Harris to death to have a whole bunch of people busting in to rescue him. It wouldn't help Earleen, either. He didn't want to chance her getting spooked and taking off.

He was going to play by the rules this time and let Hodges make the call. Dogs were barking wildly in the background when the lieutenant answered the phone.

"It's me," said Marcus. "I've found out where the boy is."

"You gonna tell me?"

"The Dew Drop Inn in Vidalia—just across the river."

"Great! That's in—" There was a pause. "Damn, in Louisiana...right?"

The dogs barked louder while Hodges digested the news. Marcus heard jumbled voices in the background and Hodges yelling, "I don't care what the sheriff said. Get that flea-bitten hair ball out of my face, right now."

Marcus grinned, happy not to be there. "I'm about to leave and go get him."

"Is there any chance Gregor knows where they are?"

"No, I don't see how he could. You want me to call the Vidalia police?"

There was a long pause. The dogs continued their frenzied barking in the background. Gradually, things got quieter. He heard more shouting and a car door slammed.

"No, Marcus, I don't want to get in a pissing contest with Vidalia's Chief of Police, too. There's enough ego to deal with here already. Just go. Get the kid and bring him back. We'll straighten out the politics after we catch Gregor. You clear?"

"Crystal."

"Perfect."

This was exactly what he'd hoped Hodges would say. The lieutenant didn't want the jurisdictional headaches; Marcus didn't want the company. He snapped the phone shut and hurried back to borrow a car from one of the Natchez officers.

CHINK. Clink.

Cally shot straight up in bed. *What was that?*

She strained to listen. Rain drummed steadily on the roof, pelting the window. The imagined noise must have been from her dream. The nap hadn't been peaceful.

She'd been in the river.

Alone.

Surrounded by water moccasins—their thick, serpent bodies wrapping around her arms and legs as she swam for shore. Jamie appeared in a boat, shaking his head *no* as she cried for help. Then Gregor's laugh and Marcus calling her name.

She scrubbed her hands across her face to clear the images and glanced at the clock. A quarter to noon. She'd slept two and a half hours.

Her entire body ached from her adventures in the real river and on shore. She felt groggy and heavy from sleep, but the memory of Marcus's hands on her body and what he'd done to her had flashes of heat shifting low in her belly. Feelings she hadn't had since before Harris was born. That she could think of sex now, while her son was missing, was on one hand horrifying and on the other, amazing. She shook her head and reached to turn on the bedside lamp. A slip of paper lay propped against a cold cup of tea.

Gone to town with Bay. Grocery-shopping and checking on Kevin at the hospital. Back after twelve. EAT SOME-THING! There's beef stew on the stove. Love L

Cally smiled.

Chink. Clink.

There it was again. Like the tinkling of wind chimes. Tiny hairs stood at attention on the back of her neck and a cold tingle skittered down her spine. Was she really alone in the house?

Cinching the white terry robe tightly around herself, she slid from the bed and scanned the room for her purse. Something wasn't right. She heard that sound again. It wasn't wind chimes, but the distinct sound of glass shattering.

She spotted her handbag in a slipper chair across the room. The .38 Special was still in there. She'd never touched it after they took Harris.

She reached for the bedside phone but knew with a sick sense of dread that the line would be dead.

Gregor is here. She could absolutely feel him. She ripped the gun from her purse as the sound of splintering glass echoed from the front of the house.

What was he doing? How had he gotten back?

Then it dawned on her. He had to have come from off the river onto the lake. That was probably the reason he'd stayed here in the first place—river access.

Icy fear coursed through her veins. Her heart pounded as she tried to swallow the lump in her throat. *Okay, calm down and think. He may not realize I'm here.*

She snuck down the hall to the kitchen. The antiseptic smell of bleach still lingered over the scent of Luella's stew. The flagstone floor chilled her bare feet; but she barely noticed as she stood, totally focused on the kitchen door, listening.

GREGOR STOOD in front of the demolished gun cabinet. For a moment he wasn't sure how he'd gotten here. He looked around the library, breathing hard, holding the fire poker so tightly his knuckles were white. The room was trashed. Several photograph frames—the pictures twisted and torn—lay on the floor alongside papers, broken glass and pottery.

Damn. That felt good. Once he'd started breaking the cabinet's leaded glass doors to get to the guns, he couldn't stop.

He hadn't been this wired since he'd put that hooker in the hospital. Stupid bitch hadn't realized who she was dealing with. But he'd given her something to remember him by.

He wiped spittle off his chin with the back of his sleeve and gingerly replaced the poker in its stand before choosing the Magnum. In search of ammo, he pulled out drawers at the bottom of the broken cabinet and took deep gulps of air. He noticed the faintest smell of something cooking—beef stew. His stomach rumbled.

He loaded the shells, looked at his dive watch and decided five more minutes to grab some food was a good use of time. It might be a while before he could stop again.

He picked his way across the littered floor, his feet making wet sucking sounds on the carpet.

CALLY STRAINED to hear over the rain pummeling the roof. Which way should she go? Should she make a run for the car? She stopped and gazed at the downpour.

What am I doing? Am I crazy?

For a moment she convinced herself there was no one else in the house.

Then she heard it. The steady "squish, squish" of someone walking toward the kitchen door.

She froze. Nowhere to hide.

The footsteps came closer.

She forced herself to move. Scurrying behind the door, she hunkered down and watched it slowly swing open.

Chapter Twenty

Rap. Rap. Rap.

Marcus stood alone outside the no-tell motel. He heard the television and a child's soft weeping through the paper-thin door. Earleen cautiously answered on the third knock.

"Who's there?"

"Marcus. Open up."

The door opened a little at a time. Earleen was a big woman with wide hips and a generous bosom. She had put on quite a bit of weight since her Farish Street days in Jackson.

Her worried expression lightened when she saw Marcus's face. "I am so glad to see you."

Sitting on the bed, Harris stared at the TV with tears running down his cheeks—sucking his thumb. Big Bird danced across the screen.

"Momma. I want Momma." The words were repeated like a litany.

"He's been crying like that since Carlotta dropped him off." She stood to the side, wearily rubbing the back of her neck. "I couldn't do nothing with him."

"Uh-huh." Marcus brushed past her and stifled his first impulse to pick Harris up and hustle him out to the car. Instead he looked around.

The room was surprisingly immaculate. He suspected Earleen had been doing some nervous cleaning while she waited. This kind of establishment never looked immaculate. Poor girl. She couldn't do much, but she'd sanitized this nasty room to within an inch of its life.

He started to say something, but thought better of it and sat down beside Cally's son.

"Hey, Harris. How ya' doin'?"

The boy turned to him with tear-swollen eyes and Marcus's heart broke a little.

"Mr. Nowth." His face lit up with a teary smile and he launched himself at Marcus's chest. "Want go home. Want go home."

Marcus's chest tightened again when Harris grasped him around the neck and laid his cheek against his. He was toast.

"Pleeease take home."

"That's where we're going, buddy, just as fast as we can." He wrapped his arms around Harris and was rewarded with a smacking kiss on the cheek. A lump of emotion rose in his throat.

"Thank you, Mr. Nowth."

He stood, carrying the child and glanced around the room to find the car seat. Earleen had slipped out while he and Harris talked.

"You got everything, partner?" The boy nodded.

Marcus snagged his car seat and headed for the police cruiser with Harris in his arms. Earleen stood in the breezeway studying the empty swimming pool that likely hadn't seen chlorinated water in over a decade.

Together they scrutinized the cracked pool as if it was the Trevi Fountain. "You're gonna take care of all the legal stuff, right, Marcus?"

He sighed. "Yeah. I'll take care of it."

Finally he looked at her, felt his own eyes tearing up. His voice was unsteady. "Thank you."

Earleen met his gaze and nodded. "I owed you."

"Not anymore." He wanted to say something to her about past

mistakes not determining her future—but he didn't. She'd put her past behind her better than he had. "You take care of yourself."

"Oh, I will. I always do." She flashed him a sad smile before he walked away.

Harris rested his head on Marcus's shoulder as they walked across the parking lot. Only when they got to the car did he loosen his grasp around Marcus's neck. Marcus strapped Harris and his car seat in and started the engine.

"Ride in police car." Harris bounced up and down despite the seat belt. "Whoo. Whoo. I like siren."

"You do? Well, I think we could manage a little siren action for this occasion."

He grinned at the boy in the rearview mirror, and found himself staring into cornflower-blue eyes identical to Cally's. His throat constricted.

What was he going to do about that? If he thought about it for too long, he might imagine himself halfway in love with this boy's mother.

"Ready to blow this Popsicle joint?"

Harris giggled and nodded enthusiastically. "I like Popsicles."

"Me, too." Marcus turned on the lights but no sirens as they eased out of the parking lot.

CALLY SCRUNCHED UP, making herself as small as possible when Gregor pushed the door open. Silently, she watched him stalk across the kitchen straight to the stove. His right arm was in a sling and Jamie's .357 was in his holster.

She slid around the door to sneak out, but her reflection caught in the glass front of the oven.

"Hello, Mrs. Burnett. I see you made it out of the river safe and sound."

He hadn't turned around yet, so he couldn't see the gun in her hand. She tucked it behind her in the folds of her robe.

Cally swallowed hard before answering. "I see the same is true for you."

"Not exactly." He turned to face her and rasped that ugly laugh as if there was some private joke. She didn't really want to know what he meant, but she had to play for time.

"What happened to the others?" she asked.

"They're dead. All dead. The idiots. The money's mostly gone, too. But I see you made it just fine. Just fine, indeed."

He leaned against the counter, brazenly looking her up and down with a malevolent smile.

Inwardly, she recoiled. Outwardly, she kept her voice steady—her expression calm. "Yes, yes I did."

She tightened her grip on the gun. Her palms were starting to sweat. *God, don't let me drop this thing.* The thought was a prayer.

"Where is my son?"

"Haven't found him yet, huh? I would've thought your cop boyfriend would have it all figured out by now."

His eyes were lit from within like they'd been at the casino. Only this time she could clearly identify the insanity.

Exhaling softly, she ground her teeth against her bottom lip. He watched as she pulled the gun from behind her back, yet he made no move to stop her.

"Tell me where he is, you sick son of a bitch, or I'll kill you." Willing her hands not to shake, she raised the revolver to point directly at his chest.

Gregor shook his head and nonchalantly turned back to the stove. "Nah, you won't kill me. You've got too much to lose."

He began ladling stew, balancing the dish between his chest and the sling. Cally stood in shock while he ignored her and the gun. After a moment she tried another tack.

"You're right, he's everything to me. That's why I'm risking everything right now. Tell me where he is, or I'll shoot you. I swear, I will."

She'd come closer as she spoke, pointing the gun at the

center of his back. Too late, she realized her mistake. He lashed out with his foot, knocking her to the ground and the .38 from her hand.

She heard the bowl hit and watched pieces of broken china skitter across the tile after her gun. When she looked up again, Gregor was holding Jamie's revolver. The barrel of the Magnum was less then two inches from her forehead.

"Mrs. Burnett, that was extraordinarily foolish. And I've had all the foolishness I can deal with today." He looked at the puddle of stew at his feet and sighed.

"Stand up, damn it."

She pulled herself off the floor. Gregor leered when he saw the way the robe had slipped from her shoulder when she fell.

He seemed to be making a decision as he stared at the white material bunched at her elbow. She swallowed audibly.

"Scared? You should be. I'm unbelievably angry with you." His voice was calm, quiet. He could have been commenting on the weather.

She forced herself to look into his eyes and wished she hadn't. They'd gone completely dead. This was far more frightening than what she'd seen earlier.

He glanced over his shoulder at the stew before turning back to her. "I'm not as hungry as I thought."

He stepped closer and pushed her into the counter, using the muzzle of the gun to open her robe. The terry cloth caught on her other elbow, completely exposing her chest and right side from shoulder to foot. She looked down at the shards of china around her feet, refusing to meet his eyes.

He used the barrel of the gun to trace a line from her throat to her breast. He slid the muzzle back and forth over her nipple and smiled when her body reacted to the friction.

"Amazing the response one can get from a woman who has been celibate for a while. You're quite different from the ladies I usually entertain."

He pressed the gun into her flesh and she gasped. He laughed and released the pressure.

"Of course, I'm not sure. Could be Marcus got here before me."

He laughed softly and continued tracing a line with his gun down over her ribs and stomach. When he reached the top of her pelvis he stopped.

"You'd do anything to save your son, wouldn't you?"

She looked at him then, nodding. A solitary tear slid down her cheek.

He smiled. It chilled her as nothing he'd done so far had. "You're going to get quite an education."

She closed her eyes to prepare herself for what she knew to be coming. The force of the blow whipped her body to the side when he struck her in the face with the gun.

At first, she felt nothing. Then she tasted the blood. Pain roared through her head. Her vision went black around the edges; she heard a loud buzzing sound.

He flattened his hips against her and held the gun to her temple. His erection pressed against her stomach. Bile rose in the back of her throat.

She closed her eyes again and concentrated on the sound of the steadily beating rain. Amazingly, she heard his stomach growl.

He ground himself against her and pushed the gun behind her ear. His stomach rumbled again. He sighed in disgust.

"Oh…screw this. Get me something to eat."

He pulled the gun from her head and stepped back, motioning angrily toward the stainless-steel pot. "*Now,* damn it. I'm hungry."

She sagged against the counter and started to close the robe. Her hands trembled as she forced her fingers to grasp the belt. Would her legs even support her?

"No, leave it."

Cally froze, dropping the edge of the sash before heading to the cabinets.

He stood by the stove, watching her get another dish. She

ladled stew, trying to think over the pounding in her head. He was going to finish what he'd started after he ate. Then he'd kill her or at least make her wish she were dead.

Think, woman, think. You've got to do something.

She limped to the sink, exaggerating her injury, and plucked a spoon from the dish-drainer. Her lip was bleeding but her head was starting to clear. She needed a little more time to get her bearings.

He held the Magnum in his left hand and his right arm was in a sling. He would have a problem eating and holding a gun on her at the same time.

Without looking up, she set the steaming bowl down beside him along with the spoon. If only she could distract him while the gun was on the counter.

"Get me something to drink."

She hobbled to the refrigerator and picked up a gallon of milk. Holding it in both hands, she tried to judge its worth as a weapon.

"Milk all right?" she whispered.

He nodded, laid the gun on the counter and picked up the spoon. She'd been waiting for that. Without hesitation she heaved the full container directly at his head.

He started to deflect it, but that arm was in a sling. All he could do was howl in rage as he stepped backward to avoid getting hit in the head. The plastic jug struck the oven door behind him, showering his upper body with cold milk.

Cally dashed out the kitchen door and took the service stairs at an Olympic-paced sprint. She didn't want to stay inside the house, but the side entrance lock was deadbolted. Gregor would have a clear shot if she ran straight to the front door.

All this had rushed through her mind as she watched the milk jug lob through the air. When she hit the first landing, a bullet whizzed past her ear—obliterating part of the window casing. She ducked her head but never slowed down, running past the elevator and up to the attic.

Gregor bellowed behind her. He was on the service stairs as she locked the door to Marcus's room.

The ladder!

Flying to the window seat, she wrestled with the curtains and shoved the window open. She pulled back the wooden top of the seat and stopped.

If she left the window up, he would think she'd gone outside. She surveyed the trunk-size rectangular box.

A tight squeeze, but I can fit.

She grabbed the ladder. With shaking hands, she slammed the lid and attached the metal and rope hooks to the window-sill. Rain blew into her face as she arranged the rungs outside.

She heard him shouting on the attic stairs—the cosmopolitan veneer completely gone. "You crazy bitch! I'm gonna kill you!"

He would, too. She remembered the deadly look in his eyes.

She again threw open the seat and stepped inside. Lying on the dusty floor, she curled into a semi-fetal position. She lowered the lid as the bedroom door splintered. Gregor was breaking through.

Chapter Twenty-One

Marcus sped through the pouring rain. The misting sprinkle that had begun when he pulled out of the hotel parking lot had built into a full-blown storm. Lightning put on a fabulous show, but Harris was missing it all.

The poor kid had fallen asleep before they'd crossed the bridge at Natchez. Marcus was anxious to get him home to Cally. She had to be frantic by now.

He'd tried to reach her through the police dispatcher, but they reported her phone out of order. He assumed the lines were down due to the weather.

He was anxious to see her. There were things he had to tell her—about himself, his work.

He turned into River Trace's long graveled drive. The ride had taken almost an hour. Harris was still dead to the world. The wind was blowing the rain so hard, he almost didn't see the open front door until he parked.

Watching water blow into the house onto the oriental carpet and oak flooring, Marcus felt the same bad mojo prickling sensation on the back of his neck he'd had at Donny's, the night he'd gotten shot.

Pulling Sydney's borrowed .38 from his shoulder holster, he peered through the windshield and snatched up the radio handset. No one answered his call for backup. But this was a

Natchez cruiser and amidst all the confusion of a multi-jurisdictional operation going on, there was no telling where the calls were being routed through, especially with the storm.

He couldn't wait long for a response. The rain came in torrents as the squeaking windshield wipers fought a losing battle. He studied the front porch through sheets of water. He heard what sounded like distant thunder.

But it wasn't the storm he was hearing. His blood chilled when he recognized the sound of a gunshot.

Pressing the handset, he spoke into the microphone, "Shots fired at River Trace, Burnett residence. Officer on scene needs assistance."

He hoped to hell they heard him. He glanced in the rearview mirror. Harris was still sleeping.

Not waiting for a reply from dispatch he dropped the radio, opened the car door and ran.

GREGOR STOOD in the wreckage of the smashed door looking wildly about the bedroom. Breathing hard, he scanned the short hallway leading to the bath and focused on the open window across the room. The rain blew in on the window seat, soaking the curtains. He strode to the seat, knelt on top and rested his good arm on the side of the windowsill.

Leaning out, he was immediately blinded by the whirling water and lightning. When his eyes were able to focus again he looked down and saw the ladder hanging into...nothingness. It was a five-foot drop from the bottom rung to the sunroof.

Hell. She's climbed out the damn window. He wouldn't have thought her that gutsy.

He was so enraged he didn't even stop to think about how he would get down the ladder with his arm. Just that he must. She was the reason this had all gone so wrong, and he was going to make her pay.

Her fault the robbery hadn't gone as planned. Cally Burnett

and Marcus North. That damn cop. If she hadn't fallen out of the boat, Sams might still be alive. Marcus would have helped pull him back onboard. Shit. They might even still have most of the money.

The wind blasted rain in his face when he moved to go after her. Over the howling storm came the faint wail of police sirens. He stopped to listen as the cacophony became louder.

Damn it. There was more than one car. This was what he'd been afraid of. And it was all that woman's fault. What should he do?

He looked back over his shoulder. A flash of white caught his eye. A tiny piece of white terrycloth stuck up, caught between the hinge and the lid.

Cally's robe.

The bitch thought she could outsmart me?

Noiselessly, he eased off the wooden top and stood in front of the window seat—training his gun on the lid.

CALLY HEARD Gregor's harsh breathing as he crawled onto the seat. The wood creaked when he moved. Lying on her side, she willed herself to stay calm. She tried to think of something besides the man on the boards above her head.

Dust filled her nostrils. *This thing hasn't been cleaned in ages.* She held her breath and concentrated on not sneezing when his boots scraped across the top.

The wood gave another mighty creak. Then it was silent.

Cally waited.

Nothing happened.

Above the wind she heard the whine of multiple police sirens. Relief washed over her. He'd gone for it and help was on the way.

She lay still. How long will it take him to get down the ladder? She wasn't sure with his arm in a sling. But she couldn't wait too long. In no time at all he'd figure out that she wasn't on the roof.

She was putting her hand up to raise the lid when it flew open. Gregor towered over her, pointing one of Jamie's guns directly at her head.

She saw his finger pulling back on the trigger. There wasn't even time to shout "*No!*" before the world exploded.

Gunfire roared into the room.

Cally screamed.

Gregor fired one shot into the floor beside her head. The sound was deafening. Wood chips flew up, stinging her face.

Gregor gazed at her with a puzzled expression—then looked to a small trickle of blood seeping from his chest. He opened his mouth to say something. Instead of words, blood poured out and he crumpled to the floor.

Cally lay curled in the bottom of the window seat. It was deathly quiet. She couldn't hear sirens anymore. She couldn't even hear the rain.

Suddenly Marcus was there, leaning over the side and pulling her into his arms. She knew he was talking to her because she could see his lips moving. She just couldn't understand him. Then she realized she couldn't hear anything at all.

He was kissing her lips and forehead. Her ears were ringing; blood was running down her cheek where the wood chips had hit her. Marcus held her, dabbing her face with his shirttail—all the while trying to make her understand what he was saying. Something about Harris.

A police officer burst in. Then another. Marcus spoke to one of the officers who quickly backed out of the room. She felt his lips pressing a kiss into her hair.

More policemen swarmed in—all wearing different uniforms. Everyone was talking at once.

Cally still couldn't make out what they were saying. It sounded like the faint buzzing of a beehive.

But that didn't matter when the man Marcus had sent away returned. He was carrying Harris—asleep and wrapped in a yellow poncho. Before she could scramble to her feet, the officer was putting her son in her arms.

The nightmare was over.

Epilogue

It was time for him to leave. He knew that.

In the growing darkness, Cally relaxed before the stone fireplace cuddling Harris in the rocking chair. Marcus sat beside them in the loveseat, grateful for the dim light. She couldn't see his eyes this way, but he could still watch her.

He'd come so close to losing her. How could he leave?

She'd doggedly refused to go to the hospital or any police station. An EMT had worked on her face and her ears. They'd thoroughly checked out Harris, too.

What was he going to do with himself now that it was over?

Several men stirred about in the kitchen. Marcus had had quite enough of them—an FBI agent, Hodges, two task-force officials, plus the county sheriff from McCay County and Vidalia's mayor. More officers were scattered throughout the house still gathering evidence. Luella had made enough coffee to keep an army of narcoleptics awake.

"Momma, rock Harris."

Cally didn't reply, she just kicked into "rock" mode, humming as the chair creaked on the stone floor. Harris laid his head on her shoulder.

Hodges motioned to Marcus from the kitchen doorway. Reluctantly, he followed his boss into the foyer.

"What have you got?" asked Marcus.

"We found Boggs's girlfriend, Carlotta. She showed up at Manny's Tonk about thirty minutes ago."

"You pressing charges?"

"Dunno. We'll have to see what the governor's man says."

"She wasn't exactly the mastermind," said Marcus.

"Yeah. We found Boggs's body about a mile south of Palmers on the Mississippi side. Haven't gotten an official ID. But we're sure it's him. They've also found two duffel bags stuffed with cash. They were hung up in some brush along the riverbank."

"No telling how much sank to the bottom. Any word on Sams?"

Hodges shook his head. "From what you described, he could be anywhere. He'll probably show up further downriver."

"Yeah," agreed Marcus, looking back to the closed door—toward Cally and Harris.

"How's Mrs. Burnett?"

He turned to Hodges. "She's going to be okay. Her hearing came back this afternoon along with a horrific headache."

Hodges shook his head. "Blast that close will do that. She was damn lucky." There was an awkward silence.

"Marcus, what are you planning to do?"

"About?"

"About the Internal Affairs investigation."

"Nothing."

"Are you going to testify?"

"No. I'm gonna quit." Marcus was surprised at how easily those words came.

Hodges sighed, "Damn. I hate to see you do that. You know they can force you to testify."

"They aren't going to want me to. Not after they hear what I tell you."

Hodges raised an eyebrow.

"It will probably affect how IA conducts their investigation or at least my participation in their investigation.

"Okay, you've got my attention."

"You remember the informant who died in the Simmons bust?" Hodges nodded. "Tessa Durbin."

"I slept with her the night before the raid, and I never told you or anyone about it. My being involved in this investigation is wrong on multiple levels. I quit, Hodges. I can't do this anymore."

The lieutenant studied him for a moment. "Is Tessa Durbin the real reason you're quitting?"

"She'll be reason enough, as far as Internal Affairs is concerned."

"Screw IA. I don't want to lose you, Marcus. You're too good at what you do. The situation with Tessa—it can happen when you're working undercover. I know that."

Marcus shook his head. "But that's just it. I don't want to do this anymore. My heart's not in it. Not like it needs to be for the job. I've got to do something else while I still can."

He glanced into the kitchen as the door swung open and stuck. Bay nodded as he passed them. Marcus's eyes were drawn to Cally and Harris in the rocking chair.

"Is there anything I can say to change your mind?" asked Hodges.

"No."

"What are you planning?" Hodges asked for the second time. Marcus was still staring at Cally and turned back to him.

"About that?" Hodges nodded toward the rocker and its occupants.

Marcus smiled faintly. *So the man was a detective after all.* "I'm not sure, but I'm working on it. I'll let you know."

"You do that."

Marcus shook his hand. "I'll get you my badge and letter of resignation tomorrow."

"Take care of yourself."

Marcus nodded and headed back into the kitchen, surprised at how simple completely changing his life had been. He wasn't sure how he felt yet, having just resigned. And he still had no plan, but he had an idea.

He stopped at the counter for coffee before he went back to Cally. She'd changed into jeans and a faded T-shirt. A bandage covered her cheek. Her lip was swollen, and she was going to have a hell of a black eye.

He wanted to kill Gregor all over again for that. His hands trembled when he thought again of how close he'd come to losing her.

Her auburn hair curled around her battered face like a halo. Harris dozed on her shoulder. She smiled lopsidedly up at him when he handed her the steaming cup. He'd fixed her coffee the way she liked, lots of cream and sugar.

"What happens now?" she asked.

With a jolt, Marcus realized he'd been staring while she was asking the question of the hour.

"These people should be clearing out pretty soon. And…you'll get your house back." He sat on the loveseat in what he was coming to think of as his "spot." Luella washed more dishes.

"That's not what I meant."

"No?"

"No." She studied him intently. "I meant what are *you* going to do now?"

"My former boss just asked me that."

"Former boss?" She stopped rocking.

He nodded, gazing out the window. "Yeah, I quit."

"Why?"

"A lot of reasons." He turned to face her, took a deep breath and dove off the cliff.

"I hate my job. It's changed me. I don't like what I've become working undercover.

"Six months ago I slept with an informant. She died in a drug bust the next day, and I didn't tell anyone about that relationship until tonight. Those actions on my part represent a serious breach of conduct."

Cally didn't turn away as he spoke what he'd come to think of as damning words. She just kept listening. He was shocked at the lack of condemnation in her eyes. She wasn't judging, even now when she'd heard the worst.

Luella dumped more dishes in the sink. He heard the water running, heard the low murmur of the officers' voices, heard the steady drumming rain—all those sounds filled the moment.

With absolute clarity he realized this was exactly where he wanted to be. Right here. Sitting beside this woman who felt like...home. If he would be known, it would be here. If there was something more, he'd find it with her. He took another deep breath.

"The real reason I quit is...you. You changed everything for me."

"Oh," She blinked and her blue eyes widened.

He kept going before he lost his nerve. "This is as real as I get, Cally. It's not an act. If you're thinking of running, now would be a good time."

"I told you at the river, I don't run."

He shook his head in disbelief. "In that case, do you think I could have a job? I'd really like to learn the catering business."

A secret smile spread across her face and the dimples were back—full force. She didn't hesitate. "I believe we could work something out."

Marcus exhaled, his eyes never leaving hers. He couldn't say anything else, so he sat there taking it all in.

Harris raised his head. "Momma, sing."

"Just a second, baby." She pressed a kiss to the boy's cheek and stood with the child in her arms to settle beside Marcus on the loveseat.

He studied her a moment, still not believing this could be his life. He slid his arm around them both and kissed her, heedless of everything and everyone. When he pulled back, he glanced down to see Harris·grinning at him.

Marcus grinned, too, tucked Cally and Harris closer, and closed his eyes as she began to hum.

"Hush, little baby, don't say a word. Momma's gonna buy you a mockingbird..."

* * * * *

*Harlequin Intrigue top author Delores Fossen presents
a brand-new series of breathtaking romantic suspense!*
TEXAS MATERNITY: HOSTAGES
*The first installment available May 2010:
THE BABY'S GUARDIAN*

Shaw cursed and hooked his arm around Sabrina.

Despite the urgency that the deadly gunfire created, he tried to be careful with her, and he took the brunt of the fall when he pulled her to the ground. His shoulder hit hard, but he held on tight to his gun so that it wouldn't be jarred from his hand.

Shaw didn't stop there. He crawled over Sabrina, sheltering her pregnant belly with his body, and he came up ready to return fire.

This was obviously a situation he'd wanted to avoid at all cost. He didn't want his baby in the middle of a fight with these armed fugitives, but when they fired that shot, they'd left him no choice. Now, the trick was to get Sabrina safely out of there.

"Get down," someone on the SWAT team yelled from the roof of the adjacent building.

Shaw did. He dropped lower, covering Sabrina as best he could.

There was another shot, but this one came from a rifleman on the SWAT team. Shaw didn't look up, but he heard the sound of glass being blown apart.

The shots continued, all coming from his men, which meant it might be time to try to get Sabrina to better cover. Shaw glanced at the front of the building.

So that Sabrina's pregnant belly wouldn't be smashed against the ground, Shaw eased off her and moved her to a sitting position so that her back was against the brick wall. They were close. Too close. And face-to-face.

He found himself staring right into those sea-green eyes.

How will Shaw get Sabrina out?
Follow the daring rescue and the heartbreaking
aftermath in THE BABY'S GUARDIAN by Delores Fossen,
available May 2010 from Harlequin Intrigue.

® **HARLEQUIN**®

INTRIGUE®

HARLEQUIN *Presents*

Bestselling Harlequin Presents® author

Lynne Graham

introduces

VIRGIN ON HER WEDDING NIGHT

Valente Lorenzatto never forgave Caroline Hales's
abandonment of him at the altar. But now he's
made millions and claimed his aristocratic Venetian
birthright—and he's poised to get his revenge.
He'll ruin Caroline's family by buying out their
company and throwing them out of their mansion...
unless she agrees to give him the wedding night
she denied him five years ago....

**Available May 2010
from Harlequin Presents!**

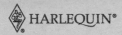
HARLEQUIN®

Showcase

On sale May 11, 2010

Reader favorites from the most talented voices in romance

Save $1.00 on the purchase of 1 or more Harlequin® Showcase books.

SAVE $1.00 on the purchase of 1 or more Harlequin® Showcase books.

Coupon expires Oct 31, 2010. Redeemable at participating retail outlets. Limit one coupon per purchase. Valid in the U.S.A. and Canada only.

52609015

5 65373 00076 2   (8100)0 11651

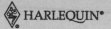 HARLEQUIN®

INTRIGUE

COMING NEXT MONTH

Available May 11, 2010

#1203 HER BODYGUARD
Bodyguard of the Month
Mallory Kane

#1204 HITCHED!
Whitehorse, Montana: Winchester Ranch
B.J. Daniels

#1205 THE BABY'S GUARDIAN
Texas Maternity: Hostages
Delores Fossen

#1206 STRANDED WITH THE PRINCE
Defending the Crown
Dana Marton

#1207 STRANGER IN A SMALL TOWN
Shivers
Kerry Connor

#1208 MAN UNDERCOVER
Thriller
Alana Matthews

HICNMBPA0410